SO MUCH FOR
THAT WINTER

Also by Dorthe Nors in English

Karate Chop

A PUBLIC SPACE BOOK

So Much for That Winter

NOVELLAS

Dorthe Nors

*Translated from the Danish
by* Misha Hoekstra

Graywolf Press

This publication is made possible, in part, by the voters of Minnesota through a Minnesota State Arts Board Operating Support grant, thanks to a legislative appropriation from the arts and cultural heritage fund, and through a grant from the Wells Fargo Foundation Minnesota. Significant support has also been provided by Target, the McKnight Foundation, the Amazon Literary Partnership, and other generous contributions from foundations, corporations, and individuals. To these organizations and individuals we offer our heartfelt thanks.

The author and the translator wish to thank the Danish Arts Foundation, the Danish Arts Council, and Hald Hovedgaard for their support.

DANISH ARTS FOUNDATION

Published by Graywolf Press
250 Third Avenue North, Suite 600
Minneapolis, Minnesota 55401

All rights reserved.

www.graywolfpress.org

Published in the United States of America

ISBN 978-1-55597-742-9

33614057662156

2 4 6 8 9 7 5 3 1
First Graywolf Printing, 2016

Library of Congress Control Number: 2015953715

Cover design: Carol Hayes
Cover art: Robert Daly / Getty Images

Contents

SO MUCH FOR
THAT WINTER

Minna Needs Rehearsal Space

Minna introduces herself.

Minna is on Facebook.

Minna isn't a day over forty.

Minna is a composer.

Minna can play four instruments.

Minna's lost her rehearsal space.

Minna lives in Amager.

Minna spends her days in the Royal Library.

Minna has to work without noise.

Minna's working on a paper sonata.

The paper sonata consists of tonal rows.

Minna writes soundless music.

Minna is a tad avant-garde.

Minna has a tough time explaining the idea to people.

Minna wants to have sound with the music—no,

Minna just wants to have sound.

Minna wants to have Lars.

Minna's in love with Lars.

Lars used to really like Minna.

Minna doesn't dare launch the relationship app.

Lars has a full beard.

Lars has light-colored curls.

Lars works for the paper.

Lars is a network person.

Lars is Lars, Minna thinks, fumbling with the duvet cover.

It's morning.

Lars has left again.

Lars is always in a hurry to get out of bed.

The bed is a snug nest.

Minna's lying in it, but

Lars is on his bike and gone.

Lars bikes as hard as he can in the direction of City
    Hall Square.

Lars makes the pigeons rise.

Lars has deadlines.

Minna has an itch on her face.

Minna goes out to the bathroom to check.

Lars has kissed her.

Minna doesn't look like who she looked like when she
    made the spaghetti last night.

Minna looks like someone who drank all the wine herself.

Minna walks around in bare feet.

The apartment is full of notes.

Bach stands in the window.

Brahms stands on the coffee table.

The apartment's too small for a piano, but

A woman should have room for a flute.

A woman should have room for a flute, a triangle, and
    a guitar.

Minna takes out the guitar.

Minna plays something baroque.

Minna plays as quietly as possible.

The neighbor bangs on the wall with his sandals.

Minna needs a rehearsal space.

Minna needs security in her existence.

Minna misses the volume.

Minna misses a healthier alternative.

Minna wants to devote herself to ecology.

Minna wants to involve a kid in it.

Minna wants to try to be just like the rest.

Lars ought to help her but

Lars uses condoms.

Lars is on his bike and gone.

Lars is Lars.

———

Minna calls Lars.

Minna calls Lars until he picks up the phone.

Minna and Lars have discussed this before.

Lars has a cousin.

The cousin's name is Tim.

Tim knows of a rehearsal space in Kastrup.

The rehearsal space is close to the airport.

The rehearsal space is cheap.

Minna's never met Tim.

Minna is in many ways desperate.

Minna says, *I can't go on being quiet.*

Minna says, *I've got to be able to turn myself up and down.*

Lars sighs.

Minna says, *Let's bike out to the rehearsal space.*

Lars doesn't want to.

Lars is a culture reporter.

Lars and Minna met at a reception.

Lars introduced himself with his full name.

Minna could see that he knew everyone.

Minna could see that he would like to know everyone, but Lars doesn't traffic in favors.

Favors are for politicians, he says.

Minna says, *But it's just a rehearsal space.*

Lars says, *One day it's rehearsal space, the next . . .*

The conversation goes on like that.

Minna pesters.

Lars relents, but only a little.

Lars says that he can call up Tim.

Minna waits by the phone.

Minna changes an A string.

Minna drinks her coffee.

The phone doesn't ring.

Minna goes for a walk.

The phone doesn't ring.

The phone is dead.

Minna checks the SIM card.

The SIM card is working.

Amager Strandpark is shrouded in sea fog.

Amager Strandpark is full of architect-designed bunkers.

Amager Strandpark wants to look like Husby Dunes.

Husby Dunes used to be part of the Atlantic Wall.

Husby Dunes used to be a war zone.

Amager Strandpark makes itself pretty with a tragic backdrop.

Minna doesn't like Amager Strandpark.

Minna really likes the Sound.

Minna loves the sea, the gulls, the salt.

Minna is a bit of a water person, and now her pocket beeps.

Minna looks at her cell phone.

Lars has sent a text.

Tim's on Bornholm, it says.

Minna was prepared for something like that, but

Minna wasn't prepared for what comes next:

Lars writes, *I think we should stop seeing each other.*

Minna reads it again, but that's what it says.

Lars is breaking up via text.

Minna cannot breathe.

Minna has to sit down on an artificial dune.

Minna writes, *Now I don't understand.*

Minna calls on the phone.

There's no signal.

Minna waits for an answer.

The cell is dead, and so she sits there:

Amager Strandpark is Husby Dunes meets Omaha Beach.

Amager Strandpark is full of savage dogs trying to flush
    something out.

Amager Strandpark is a battlefield of wounded women.

————

Minna has gotten Lars to elaborate on his text.

Lars wrote, *But I'm not really in love with you.*

Lars has always understood how to cut to the chase.

Minna can't wring any more out of him.

Lars is a wall.

Lars is a porcupine.

Minna lies in bed.

The bed is the only place she wants to lie.

Minna hates that he began the sentence with *But*.

Minna feels that there was a lot missing before *But,* but

Minna should have apparently known better.

Men are also lucky that they possess the sperm.

Men can go far with the sperm.

Men with full sacks play hard to get.

Men with full sacks turn tail, but

Minna can manage without them.

Minna is a composer.

Minna feels her larynx.

The larynx isn't willing.

Minna can hear her neighbor come home.

Minna places an ear against the wall.

The neighbor dumps his groceries on the table.

The neighbor takes a leak.

Minna puts Bach on the stereo.

Minna turns up Bach.

The neighbor is there instantly.

Bach's cello suites are playing.

Minna's fingers are deep in the wound.

Minna looks at the portrait of Lars.

The portrait is from the paper.

Lars is good at growing a beard.

Lars sits there with his beard.

Lars's mouth is a soft wet brushstroke.

Chest hair forces his T-shirt upward.

The beard wanders downward away from his chin.

An Adam's apple lies in the middle of the hair.

Minna has had it in her mouth.

Minna has tasted it.

Minna has submitted, but

Lars looks out at someone who isn't her.

Lars regards his reader.

It isn't her.

Minna is tormenting herself.

Minna feels that Lars is a hit-and-run driver.

The hit-and-run driver has suffered at most a dented fender.

Minna savors her injuries.

Her heart is spot bleeding.

Her mouth stands agape.

Minna comforts herself.

Minna has the music, after all.

No one can take the music from her.

The music is an existential lifeline.

Minna would just rather have a child.

Minna ought to be glad for what she's got.

Minna would just rather have a child.

Once upon a time, composers were sufficient
      unto themselves.

Composers didn't need to have kids.

The tendency has changed:

Minna should take it upon herself to have a child.

Minna looks at the bookcase.

Minna grabs the first book under B.

Ingmar Bergman opens up for her.

Bergman's wearing the beret.

Bergman's gaze peers deep into Minna.

Bergman wants to get in under Minna's persona.

Minna's persona attempts to make way for him.

Minna wants Bergman all the way inside.

Bach plays.

The neighbor thumps.

Bergman drills.

Minna keeps all superfluous organs to the side.

Bergman says, *I am drilling, but . . .*

Either the drill breaks, or else I don't dare drill deeply enough.

Minna's managed the impossible:

Bergman can't find the woman in Minna.

The mother won't turn up.

The mother, the whore, the witch.

Minna lifts up her blouse a little.

Bergman shakes his head.

Minna stuffs him up under the blouse.

Bergman doesn't protest.

Bergman makes himself comfortable.

Bergman whispers sweet words to her.

Bergman's words don't work.

Minna's lower lip quivers.

Minna whispers, *I used to sing.*

———

Minna hasn't been out of her apartment in three days.

Minna has sent a lot of texts.

Minna has asked Lars to tell her what was supposed to be in front of *But*.

Lars doesn't reply.

Lars won't budge an inch.

Lars was otherwise so mellow.

Minna recalls when they last saw each other.

Minna and Lars lay in bed.

Minna stroked his beard.

Minna read and interpreted.

Lars just needs time.

Minna decides to send Lars an email.

Minna writes, *I think we should meet and talk about it.*

Minna writes, *We can always of course be friends.*

Minna writes, *I miss you so.*

It's wrong to write that, yet she's written it regardless.

It thunders through the ether.

The email's directional.

Minna's ashamed.

The rehearsal space is gone.

Tim's on Bornholm.

Minna's got no money.

Minna's got no boyfriend.

Minna's only got herself, and now she's going out.

Minna goes down the stairs.

Minna goes down to her bike.

The bike stands in the backyard.

The backyard amplifies all sound.

The neighbors' orgasms, the magpies, the pigeons dominate.

Minna puts on her bike helmet.

Minna bikes onto Amagerbrogade.

Minna walks through the revolving doors into the
Royal Library.

Minna wants to concentrate.

The young female students are wearing high heels.

The heels bang against the floor.

Minna despises the students' high heels.

Minna despises their catwalk character.

Minna doesn't think they've studied what they ought to.

Minna fiddles with her sonata.

Minna removes long hairs from her blouse.

Minna waits for news from Lars.

Karin's sent her an email.

Karin sends lots of emails every day.

Karin's emails are long.

Karin tells about her life in the country.

Minna's with her in the bedroom.

Minna's with her at handball in the gym.

Minna isn't shielded from anything.

Karin uses Minna as a diary.

Karin's everyday life will take over Minna's.

Minna makes a rare quick decision.

Minna writes, *Dear Karin.*

It's not you.

It's me.

Minna breaks up with Karin.

All things must have an end.

A worm has two.

Minna doesn't write the last bit.

One shouldn't hurt others unnecessarily.

One should above all be kind.

Minna would rather not be anything but.

Minna's hardly anything but.

The email thunders through the ether toward Karin.

That's as it should be, thinks Minna.

The ether is full of malicious messages.

The ether hums with breakups and loss.

The ether is knives being thrown.

The ether is blood surging back.

Minna has wounded a creature.

Minna stares out on the canal.

Minna listens to the banging heels.

Minna needs to go to the bathroom.

———

Minna's peed.

Minna's back in her place.

Minna sits and feels the pain.

The pain's a contagion.

The borders recede.

Cynicism buds.

Pointlessness grimaces!

Minna's snuck Bergman out of her bag.

Minna's got to concentrate.

Someone waves from behind the panoramic glass.

Jette's standing with a bakery bag.

Coffee's to be drunk on the quay.

Jette's a classically trained harpist.

Jette's given up finding rehearsal space.

The harp's stood in her way her entire life.

Minna knows the feeling.

Minna's had the same experience with grand pianos, but

Grand pianos grow on trees.

Harps are exclusive.

Harps are for fairies, angels, and the frigid.

Jette's erotic.

Jette calls her boyfriends *lovers.*

Jette's boyfriends are married to other women.

Jette's studying composition in Reading Room North.

Minna writes paper sonatas in Reading Room East.

Minna and Jette drink coffee together.

The relationship isn't supposed to get serious.

Jette talks too much about bodies.

Jette has an IUD in her genital tract.

Jette has discharges and domestic obligations.

Jette needs a weekend escape with a lover.

Jette fears vaginal dryness.

The uterus is an abandoned studio apartment.

The vagina's the gateway to the enjoyment of all things.

Jette says, *Don't you agree?*

Minna says, *Isn't that a balloon?*

Minna points to a spot above the harbor.

Jette's content with the two kids she has.

Enough's enough, says Jette.

Jette has two kids, thinks Minna.

Minna has a hard time getting up from the quay.

Minna feels like a horse.

Minna says, *I think it was Bugs Bunny.*

Jette goes through the door into the Royal Library.

Minna stands there like a fly in the ointment, and then she
    has to pee.

Minna has to really pee, and it has to happen fast.

———

Minna has to go to the john twice a day on average when
    she works at the Royal Library.

Minna pees.

Minna fills her water bottle from the tap.

Minna leaves the john.

Minna's surrounded by a couple hundred police officers
    in mufti.

The officers are with the Danish National Police.

The officers stand at attention in the buffet area.

The officers are at a conference in the Karen Blixen
    Meeting Room.

Minna watches the deputy commissioner eat a fish roll.

Minna slopes through the crowd.

Minna is a relic.

Minna spools up across two hundred officers.

Minna towers over four hundred sperm-filled sacs.

The officers' laughter bursts through the room.

Jens Peter Jacobsen shudders.

Hans Christian Andersen ditto.

Yard upon yard of shelving turns its back.

Minna writes tonal rows.

Minna sweats.

Minna works like a horse.

Minna heaves the tones around on the paper.

Minna clears her throat.

Minna clears her throat a little more.

The girl to her left shushes her.

Minna packs up and rides downstairs.

Minna enters the revolving doors from one side.

A police officer enters from the other.

Minna revolves around with the officer.

Minna is walking and going round.

The revolving door mechanism feels defective.

The officer gets his foot caught.

The revolving door stops heavily.

The revolving door spits Minna out like a clay pigeon.

Iceland Wharf lies far beneath Minna.

Iceland Wharf shines flat and practical.

Minna sees far beneath her the mermaid on the quay.

Minna looks out across the city.

Minna floats.

Minna's in flight over Copenhagen.

Minna's an instance of female buoyancy and helium.

———

Lars is as silent as the grave, but

Karin's answered quickly.

Minna's seated herself in her kitchen at home.

Minna doesn't dare open the email from Karin.

Karin plays accordion.

Minna and Karin took a class together.

Karin latched onto Minna.

Minna is somewhat of a host species.

Minna has now finally told Karin to stop.

The decision's good enough.

The decision was just made too late.

Karin feels bad now.

Karin's self-worth has been damaged.

Karin's self-worth is Jutlandic.

Karin brags about motocross, sex, and pork sausage.

Karin's married to a farmer.

The farmer's bought up the parish.

The parish belongs to Karin.

Karin drinks tall boys.

Karin plays folk dances.

Karin's on the gym board.

Karin sticks her hand all the way up her neighbor.

Karin grasps the inner udder.

Karin milks.

Karin pinches and squeezes.

The teat yields.

The teat's tugged long and white.

The teat grows tender and stiff.

The teat grows so tired in the end.

Minna also wrote her, *Now relax,* but

Karin doesn't need to restrain herself:

Karin goes to zumba.

Minna was right to break up with her.

A person ought to defend herself.

Minna opens the email from Karin.

Minna's right.

Karin writes nasty things about Minna.

Minna can't for example land a man.

Men don't want women like Minna.

Age will drag you down!!! Karin writes.

Barrenness will haunt you!!! Karin writes, and continues:

Minna doesn't know how to live.

Minna only knows how to think.

Karin's got everything that Minna wants.

Karin's got a dog, a man, and kids.

Karin's got five hundred acres of land.

Minna's got zilch.

Minna's lonely, a failure, and deserves to be pissed on.

Karin pisses.

Minna thinks that should suffice.

People are getting worse and worse.

Middle fingers poke out of car windows.

Small dogs shit before her entry.

Young men shout *whore*.

The three Billy Goats Gruff play havoc in nice
folks' sunrooms.

People's faces look kind.

People's faces *aren't* kind.

Minna wants to reply.

Minna wants to write nasty things too, but

Minna thinks enough's enough.

Minna longs for shut traps.

Minna longs for stillness and beauty.

Minna seats herself by the window.

Minna looks down on the street.

Minna watches a small dog gently squeeze out a turd up
onto the curbstone.

———

Night has descended on Amager.

Denmark is laid in darkness.

The Sound flows softly.

The planes take off and land.

Minna awakens.

Minna gasps.

Lars was in the dream.

Minna and Lars were at the beach.

Minna was buried with just her head free.

The sea was rough at the foot of the dune.

The sea raged, foaming white.

Dad stood in the breakers and waved.

Minna wanted to grab Lars in her haste.

Minna wriggled her arms.

The arms wouldn't budge.

Lars pelted her with sand.

Lars patted her hard with a shovel.

Lars poured water over her.

Lars used her to build a sand castle.

The wave reached land.

The wave reached land and trickled slowly.

The beads of gravel rattled.

Dad vanished.

Minna awoke.

Minna turned on the light and now it is quiet.

Amager steams with rain.

The rain refracts off the manholes.

Minna never bakes cake.

Minna gets up to bake a cake.

Minna bakes a cake in the middle of the night.

Cake is the opiate of the people.

———

Jette sits on the quay and is intimate.

Minna's brought cake for coffee.

Minna unwraps the tinfoil from a piece of cake.

The tinfoil feels childish.

The cake isn't very good either.

Jette's been to a seminar.

Jette has a new lover.

The lover's Russian.

The Russian's as hot as fresh borscht.

The Russian's French is good.

Jette's got Reds in her pleasure pavilion, thinks Minna.

Minna looks at the mermaid on the quay.

The mermaid is green.

The mermaid cannot swim.

The mermaid would sink to the bottom immediately.

Minna says, *Such sun!*

Jette says, *What about you?*

Minna says, *I'm working on the paper sonata.*

Minna knows perfectly well that Jette means sex.

Minna knows perfectly well that Jette wants to
     trade moisture.

Minna knows perfectly well that Jette's leading on points.

Karin too.

Minna understands completely.

It's something to do with physics.

It's also something to do with the soul.

Minna can't explain it.

Minna bloody won't explain it either.

Minna looks at the mermaid.

The mermaid's tail fin is cast in bronze.

The mermaid's tail fin can't slap.

The world is a suit of clothes.

The clothes too tight.

The corneas drying out.

Minna stretches: *Work calls.*

Jette says, *Leaving already?*

Minna is.

Minna disappears up to the reading room.

Minna stares at her in-box.

Everyone writes and no one answers, thinks Minna.

Elisabeth's written.

Elisabeth will treat her to a cup of tea.

Elisabeth is Minna's big sister.

Karin, Elisabeth, and Jette, thinks Minna.

Women in their prime.

Women with the right to vote.

Women with educations.

Women with their own needs.

Women with herb gardens and the pill.

Steamrollers, thinks Minna.

One mustn't think like that.

Women are awful to women, Minna's mother always said.

Mom's right, but

Women are tough to swallow.

Minna doesn't understand why men like women.

Women want to cross the finish line first.

Women want to look good on the podium.

Women are in the running, but

Minna's from another world.

Minna's a composer.

Minna's not a mother.

Minna doesn't have a mothers' group.

Minna sees the mothers' group often.

The mothers' group takes walks in Amager.

The mothers' group drives in formation.

The mothers' group is scared of getting fat.

The mothers' group goes jogging with their baby buggies.

The mothers' group eats cake at the café.

The mothers' group contends gently for the view.

The baby buggies pad the façade.

The baby buggies form a breastwork.

Minna fears the mothers' group.

Minna cannot say that out loud.

Minna has no child.

Minna can't let herself say anything.

Minna's not home free.

Minna once won a prize for some chamber music.

Minna would rather have gotten a license to live.

———

Minna has lain down on the couch.

Minna looks forward:

The prospect's hazy.

Minna looks backward:

Time has passed.

Minna recalls the Bay of Aarhus.

Minna recalls Dad:

Dad and Minna hike through Marselisborg Forest.

Dad and Minna hike down to Ballehage Beach.

Dad and Minna sniff the anemones.

Dad and Minna change into their bathing suits.

Dad and Minna position themselves on the pier.

Dad and Minna inhale the salt.

The wind's taken hold of Dad's hair.

The wind whips around Minna's ditto.

Dad and Minna stand with their arms extended.

Dad's armpits hairy.

Minna's bathing suit with balloon effect.

Dad's finger toward the horizon: *Helgenæs!*

Minna takes a running jump.

Minna shoots out into the bay.

Dad's a water bomb.

Dad and Minna dive.

Dad and Minna splash each other.

Dad and Minna can do anything, but

Minna grew up.

Minna had to bathe alone.

Minna hiked through Marselisborg Forest.

Minna wanted to hike down to Ballehage, but

Minna met a roe deer.

The deer stood on a bluff.

The deer stood stock-still and stared at Minna.

Minna stood stock-still and stared at the deer.

The deer was a creature of the deep forest.

The deer was mild and moist of gaze.

Minna was mild and moist of gaze.

The deer's legs like stalks.

The deer's fur in the sun.

Minna's hair in the wind.

The forest was empty when the deer departed.

Minna looked across the bay.

Minna inhaled the salt.

Minna gazed at the pier.

Minna picked mushrooms from half-rotted stumps.

Minna threw her arms around a beech tree.

Love ought to reassert itself.

Loss ought to do something, but

Loss and love are connected, Minna thinks.

Minna lies in Amager.

Minna turns on her side.

Love presupposes loss.

Minna deeply misses Lars.

The pain's connected to hope.

Hope is light green.

Hope is a roe deer on a bluff.

Someone has got to love, thinks Minna.

Someone's got to fight.

———

Minna's got a lot to fight.

Lars has deleted her.

Minna is no longer friends with Lars.

Lars has spoken.

Minna's been expunged.

Lars has disappeared from her wall, but

Minna can see Lars everywhere.

Lars hangs out with the others.

Lars invites people for beer.

That's awful enough.

This is worse:

Lars comments on everything Linda Lund says.

Linda Lund also attended the conservatory.

Minna was good at piano.

Linda was good at guitar, but

Linda's better suited to the music industry.

Minna can screw a reporter without getting her picture in
the paper.

Linda Lund just has to cross the street.

Linda's sex appeal is undeniable.

Minna can feel Linda's sex in everything.

Sex is power.

Sex is currency.

Linda is loaded.

The world's a stage.

The stage is Linda's.

No one may block the view of Linda.

Minna knows that.

Minna and Linda run into each other now and then.

Minna still has scars from the last time.

Minna stood there with her score.

Minna was making for the stage.

Minna was supposed to perform just like the others, but

Minna ran into Linda in the wings.

Linda pulled out a mental machete.

Linda slashed a couple times.

Linda said, *That dress will blend into the curtain.*

Linda said, *What's your name again?*

Minna almost couldn't perform afterward.

Lars is in for it.

Lars congratulates Linda on her birthday.

Linda replies, *Thanks for last night, kiss kiss.*

Lars writes, *Nice!*

Linda says, *It certainly was.*

Lars says, *Rock on, babe!*

Linda's a cannonball in jacket and skirt.

Lars is a hypnotized reporter.

Minna sits and gasps.

Karin sits on the grill of her 4x4.

Karin sits and smiles on her 4x4.

Minna unfriends vehicle and Karin both.

Minna unfriends Linda Lund too.

Minna doesn't want to be an unwilling witness!

Minna doesn't want her nose rubbed in the piss.

Minna unfriends another two people.

Minna unfriends more.

Minna unfriends Britta.

Britta's an old schoolmate.

Britta's written,

Britta's put the pork loin on the Weber.

Minna can no longer leave well enough alone, but

The unfriendings provide no relief.

Minna's been unfriended herself.

The pain of being unfriended is unbearable.

Minna misses Lars.

Lars has inflicted a trauma.

Minna's in love with someone who's traumatized her.

Minna figures that makes her a masochist.

Minna doesn't want to be a masochist.

Minna wants to be a human being, but

Minna's expunged.

It hurts so much, Minna whispers.

Minna goes in the shower.

Minna lets the water run, and then she stands there:

Minna with her lips turned toward the tiles.

Minna with blood on her hands.

Minna with soap in her eyes.

Minna with no roe deer.

———

The ringmaster of a flea circus lets the artists suck his blood.

Bergman strokes Minna on the cheek.

A daydreamer isn't an artist anywhere but in his dreams.

Bergman reaches for the buttermilk.

Bergman has indigestion.

Minna has a burnt taste in her mouth.

Bergman whispers, *I contain too much humanity.*

The days are long, large, light.

They're as substantial as cows, as some sort of bloody big animal.

Minna snuggles up to Bergman.

Dad strokes Minna's cheek.

Dad settles himself on his rock.

Dad understands.

Dad isn't scared.

———

Minna's read Bergman for a couple days.

Minna's tired of lying in bed.

Minna checks her email.

Minna's gotten a lot of email.

Mom and Jette have written.

Elisabeth's written, and look here:

Karin's written.

That was expected.

Minna doesn't know if she'll read Karin's missive.

The street clatters with bikes and cars.

The sun's risen over Amager Strandpark.

Baresso's opened.

The coffees to go are warming palms.

The coffees to go are out walking.

The cell phones, the blankies, the coffees to go.

People trickle toward City Hall Square.

People resemble shoals of shiny herring.

People press on with sand and sleep in their eyes.

Minna eats a cracker.

Karin's missive awaits.

Karin wants to be nasty.

Karin wants to upset her applecart, but

Minna's cart has no apples.

The damage has been done.

Lars has disappeared.

Linda's getting laid.

Karin has a dog.

Karin takes walks with her dog on the beach.

The dog'll fetch a stick for Karin.

The dog whips back and forth.

Karin throws farther and farther.

The dog doesn't hold back.

Karin casts the stick in the ocean.

The dog throws itself in.

Karin keeps casting the stick.

The dog keeps bounding.

It could continue this way forever, but

Minna's got to get to it.

Minna reads:

Karin's discovered that she's been unfriended.

Karin's hurt.

Karin repeats the gist from last time.

Karin just spices up the gist a bit:

Jutlandic women can fuck!!!

Music should be popular!!!

Music shouldn't be deep!!!

KARIN LOVES BRYAN ADAMS!!!

Minna swallows her cracker.

Karin keeps going: *I feel bad for you!!!*

Karin can say more: *You'll come to regret it!!!*

Minna's counted Karin's exclamation points.
The email contains fifty-six exclamation points.
That's plenty, but
Minna doesn't even feel like crying.
Minna's anesthetized to blows.
Minna looks out the window.
Minna looks down upon the transport tsunami.
The network people whiz away.
The network people have business cards.
A chink suffices.
The darkness yields willingly, but
Network hearts don't have the time.
Minna considers her hands.
Minna thinks her hands resemble thimbles.
Minna's hands *are* thimbles.
Thimbles can't grab.
The world around is laid with tile.
Network people are highly polished.
Minna shakes herself.
Minna tests her grasping power on her hair.
Her fingers can still grab herself hard.
Better than nothing, thinks Minna, and sits down.

———

Paper sonatas don't write themselves.
Minna bikes to the Royal Library.
The city's blazing hot from the sun.
The cell's blazing hot from messages.

Elisabeth's after her.

Elisabeth's ten years older than Minna.

Elisabeth's married to a successful optician.

Elisabeth lives in Potato Row.

The optician's skinny and dry.

Minna understands him.

The optician's a guest in his own home.

Guests have it rough at Elisabeth's.

Shoes have to be taken off in the hall.

Shoes must never cross the threshold.

The guest has to pee.

The guest really has to pee.

The john lies on the far side of the utility room.

The shoes have to be removed anyway.

The shoes have to be put on and taken off without leaning
  on the walls.

The walls in the hallway must not get any grimy spots.

The bench in the hallway must not have any bottoms
  upon it.

The bench is *not* to sit on.

The bench is there to create harmony in the hallway.

The guest is barefoot and entering a house full of rules.

Elisabeth makes the rules.

No one else has permission to make rules in the house.

Cutlery must not clink against the service.

The table must not be wiped with a wet rag.

Books must be bound in dust jackets.

Fingers must not touch the pictures.

The coffee mugs must not stand without coasters underneath.

The coffee mugs must not contain coffee.

Coffee is forbidden at Elisabeth's.

Everyone must drink tea.

The optician gets the trots from tea, but

The optician must remove his shoes before he runs out to
the john.

The optician struggles with his suede shoes in the hallway.

The optician is afraid to place his fingers anywhere.

The optician just reaches the toilet in his stocking feet.

The shit runs out of him like green tea.

Elisabeth shouts, *Is that you, honey?*

The shit runs and runs.

The optician considers whether he dares to shit any more.

Elisabeth shouts, *Is that you who came home, honey?*

The optician reaches for the toilet paper.

The optician remembers to tear it off in a straight line.

The optician is lonesome, completely without allies.

Elisabeth and the optician have neither dog nor kids.

It's sad, but

One thing is certain:

Kids set their bottoms everywhere.

Elisabeth is turning fifty besides.

Elisabeth is still pretty.

Elisabeth's hair is light like Minna's, but

Elisabeth's hair doesn't dare curl.

Elisabeth is illuminated.

Elisabeth is an act of will.

Elisabeth's sent Minna a stream of messages.

Minna sits on her bike and reads them.

Minna approaches Knippel Bridge.

Minna has one hand on the handlebars.

Minna has one eye on the display.

Elisabeth wants her to phone.

Elisabeth wants her to drop by.

Minna passes the Stock Exchange.

Minna holds for a bus.

Minna MUST ring between two and four.

Minna MUST NOT ring at any other time.

Elisabeth practices yoga and meditates.

The day is scheduled.

Elisabeth says it's about respecting others' needs.

Minna understands:

Lars has a need to screw a celebrity.

Jette has a need to share her sex life.

Karin has a need to take up space in the countryside.

Linda Lund has a need for an audience.

Minna has to get up to stand on the pedals.

Minna is honked at.

Minna bikes out into the intersection by the Stock Exchange.

Elisabeth pursues her.

Elisabeth was an only child for ten years.

Elisabeth's still an only child.

Elisabeth is no healthier than Karin.

Karin requires a host animal.

Elisabeth requires weak creatures.

Weak creatures can defer their needs.

Elisabeth has to be done with hers first.

Elisabeth will never be done with hers.

Elisabeth was never at Ballehage Beach either.

The sand was untidy, but

Dad and Minna could dive.

Minna's not weak.

Minna won't!

The traffic roars around Minna.

The traffic's unsafe.

Minna turns past Det Røde Palæ.

Minna bikes and taps.

Minna taps, *I'm just on my bike.*

Elisabeth orders her to call anyway.

Minna turns off her cell.

Minna drops the cell into her bag.

The bag trembles in the bike basket.

Minna trembles on the bike, but

Paper sonatas don't write themselves.

———

The quay oozes female students.

The police officers are back in Karen Blixen.

The officers stand smoking on the quay.

The officers keep an eagle eye on the students.

The students don't see the officers.

The students cast their hair about.

Their hair flips from side to side.

The students get to their feet.

The officers get to their feet.

The students' legs grow long.

The officers' pants have pockets.

The officers tug at their pockets.

The officers camouflage their sperm-filled bits.

Minna and Jette sit *sans camouflage* in the midst of it all.

Jette's eyes are insistent.

Minna has a hard time relaxing.

The legs biking.

The arms warding off blows.

The body full of vim.

The soul supposed to sit still.

It ain't easy.

Jette notices that sort of thing.

Jette says, *You seem stressed out.*

Minna replies, *I've got a little too much going on.*

Jette says, *Tell, tell!*

Minna says, *Oh, you know . . .*

Jette says, *You shouldn't walk around keeping everything bottled up.*

Minna says, *The paper sonata's bumping along.*

Minna says that she'll buy a keyboard.

Jette thinks she could just use her Mac.

Macs have a program for composers.

Macs are easy to figure out.

Minna doesn't want to say that she can't figure them out.

Minna doesn't want to satisfy Jette's need to know better.

Minna says, *It's my sister, that's all.*

Minna points at the mermaid on the quay.

The mermaid by the Royal Library is more appealing
than Langelinie's.

The mermaid by the Royal Library is anything
but charming.

The mermaid by the Royal Library can do somersaults.

The mermaid has just come ashore.

The quay is a rock.

The mermaid has a hold, but

The world makes it tough.

Anne Marie Carl-Nielsen made the mermaid.

Anne Marie Carl-Nielsen was kind to animals.

Anne Marie Carl-Nielsen was married to Carl Nielsen.

Anne Marie Carl-Nielsen was a great sculptor.

Carl Nielsen was a great composer.

Carl Nielsen wasn't an easy man to be married to, says Minna.

Carl Nielsen couldn't ignore his needs.

Carl was a firecracker.

Carl was a billy goat.

Anne Marie sculpted horses in Jutland.

Carl had ladies visit in Copenhagen.

Anne Marie's horses got bigger and bigger.

Carl's ladies got rifer and rifer.

Anne Marie placed herself beneath the horses.

Carl placed himself beneath the ladies.

Anne Marie had to learn to forgive.

Anne Marie had to stomach it.

The mermaid casts herself up out of the sea.

The mermaid contracts like a muscle before it explodes.

The mermaid clings to dry land, angry and insecure.

The mermaid is pure wet will.

She gasps.

She stares at the quay's young people.

Carl Nielsen was a handsome man, says Jette.

Carl Nielsen was stumpy, says Minna.

Carl Nielsen could've been my lover, says Jette.

The conversation's taken a familiar turn.

The Russian has a wife in Moscow.

The wife in Moscow doesn't know a thing.

Minna looks at the mermaid.

The mermaid knows all.

———

Minna's mother lives in Aarhus.

Minna's from Jutland, just like Karin.

Minna's just not from Jutland in the same way.

Minna's from Marselisborg Forest.

Minna's an old man's daughter.

Minna's a younger widow's caboose.

Mom's still a widow, but

Mom's got a boyfriend.

The boyfriend's name is Finn.

Finn and Mom go to museums.

Finn and Mom attend folk high school.

Finn and Mom each live alone.

Mom's too old for the whole package.

Finn would otherwise be interested, but

Mom's master in her own house.

Mom's also good at staying in touch.

Mom's taken a computer class at the Senior Club.

Mom's on Facebook.

Mom's got a blog.

Mom can text.

Elisabeth says you're feeling poorly, she writes.

Elisabeth's worried, she writes.

Mom's worried too.

Minna stands in the hallway and reads.

Minna considers getting a cat.

The cat'd come stealing in from the living room.

The cat'd rub up against Minna's leg.

The cat and Bergman, Minna thinks.

Minna collapses on the couch.

Bergman rests on the table.

Bergman's there for the grasping.

You'll do what's needed, he says.

Failures can have a fresh, bitter taste, he says.

Minna lays him to her breast.

Bergman makes himself at home there.

Minna closes her eyes:

Minna can hear the cars down on the street.

Minna can hear herself drawing breath.

Bergman curls up into a ball.

Minna dozes.

Minna dreams of a house on a hill.

The yard bulges with fruit and lilacs.

Phlox, mallow, iris blossoming.

The gable wall glows with English roses.

The fjord flashes at the foot of the hill.

Minna's seated on the patio.

The boats tack into the wind.

The henhouse has been whitewashed.

The henhouse is the rehearsal space.

The grand piano stands plumb in the middle.

Minna turns her face toward the sun.

Minna's chest arches over her heart.

The heart is lovely in its dissolution.

The heart has weathered the storm.

Minna listens to the interior of the house.

The door's opened and shut.

Keys are laid upon the table.

Someone's approaching the patio door.

Lars stands there smiling.

Lars bends over his woman.

Lars caresses his woman's belly.

The baby kicks inside.

The reaper-binder rattles outside.

The skylarks sing high in the air.

The rifle club's meeting in the gravel pit.

The rifle club shoots clay pigeons.

The clay pigeons whiz across the landscape.

The clay pigeons are shot or shatter when they fall.

The clay pigeons fall and fall.

Minna's wakened by a muffled thud on the floor.

It's Bergman.

It's Monday, Minna remembers.

It's all just Amager, she remembers.

———

It's a miracle.

Elisabeth's visiting Minna's apartment.

Elisabeth stands in the middle of the living room.

Elisabeth's in stocking feet.

The face as hard as enamel.

Elisabeth's rage is family legend.

The examples are legion:

Elisabeth removes bikes in Potato Row.

Nothing may shade the house.

Nothing may destroy the harmony of the façade.

Elisabeth doesn't move the bikes a couple yards.

Elisabeth walks around to other streets with the bikes.

No one should think they're safe.

Elisabeth threatens people with lawsuits and
    psychotic episodes.

Elisabeth drives people to numerologists, and even worse:

Elisabeth once made Mom have a breakdown over a piece
    of royal porcelain.

Elisabeth's aligned the stars on her side, and now she stands
    in the living room:

Dust rises: *Didn't I tell you to call?*

Elisabeth continues, *Didn't I tell you to come by?*

Minna proffers tea.

Elisabeth sets her purse down on the coffee table.

Elisabeth's eyes flit from the dirty laundry to Bach.

Elisabeth eyes need to shut for a bit.

Minna edges past her sister.

Minna pours calcified water into two mugs from IKEA.

Minna stuffs in the teabags.

Minna walks back to the living room.

Elisabeth has seated herself.

Minna sets a mug before her.

Elisabeth doesn't want the tea.

The tea ought to be green, *So why didn't you call?*

Minna doesn't manage to answer.

Elisabeth cranks up the language.

The language lashes Minna.

The language is a castigation.

Minna sips her tea.

Sisters should be there for each other, Elisabeth says.

Sisters should save each other from the muck.

Minna's life gleams with muck, *Is it that reporter?*

Minna says it might be.

Elisabeth sighs.

Elisabeth reaches out for her purse.

Minna knows what's coming: the prescription.

Elisabeth's into Ayurvedic medicine.

Ayurvedic medicine stems from India.

Ayurvedic medicine divides people into types.

Elisabeth is fire, Elisabeth says.

Minna's mud.

No one's surprised.

Elisabeth's been to the Bookstore of the Unknown.

Elisabeth's bought a book about demons.

The demons are Indian.

The book's dust jacket is black.

Elisabeth says that the book will provide Minna with fire.

Indian demons are good at rage.

Demons transform through destruction.

Minna watches her sister's face: it actually opens up.

The face is a soup pot of crazy ideas.

The sister feels certain the reporter can be exorcised.

Minna will see, it'll be a relief.

Minna looks at the book and understands.

Minna is a weak creature.

Elisabeth's stronger.

Minna thanks her.

Minna's a pleaser.

Elisabeth's rage is legend in the family, but

Elisabeth's doing better now.

Elisabeth gets up and adjusts her clothing.

A vacuum cleaner wouldn't hurt, Elisabeth says.

Minna nods.

Aarhus is still on the map, Elisabeth says.

Minna nods.

Dad got to be old as the hills.

Minna nods.

Life goes on.

Minna nods.

It's really late, her sister says.

Minna nods and nods and nods.

———

Elisabeth's demons lie on the nightstand.

Minna can't sleep.

The demons sneak about in the dark.

The demons reek of soot.

Minna switches on the light and opens the door to the
    kitchen stairs.

Minna goes down into the backyard and its twilight.

The man in number eight's watching soccer.

The woman in number four's having sex.

The stars twinkle.

The trash can gapes.

Minna casts the demons from her and closes the lid.

Minna opens the lid again.

Minna jams the book under a bag.

It's not enough.

Minna jams it farther down.

Minna can feel the trash around her hand.

Minna feels the trash's soft and hard parts.

Minna gets damp fingers.

Minna gets her upper arm in.

Minna thinks of vets and midwives.

Minna's as deep down as she can get.

Minna releases the book.

The book's wedged in there deep down.

Minna hauls back her damp arm.

Minna averts her face from the stench.

Minna presses the lid down hard.

The man in number eight scores.

The woman in number four ditto.

Minna goes back upstairs.

Minna scrubs herself.

Minna goes to bed.

Minna can't sleep.

You never know with demons.

Demons are parasites.

Parasites need individuals.

Minna knows that.

Minna's an individual herself.

Minna's one individual among millions.

Minna's a gnu on the savannah.

Minna's a herring in a barrel, but even worse:

Minna places her hands across her eyes.

Minna feels something: *Is that hair?*

Minna slips out to the mirror.

Minna places her face against it, and there she is:

Minna with fur on her face.

Minna in a wild stampede.

Minna on her way over the cliff edge.

The sea waiting below.

Death by drowning.

Her paws paddling and paddling.

The paws can't do it, they can't.

The orchestra plays a hymn.

Minna can no longer sing.

Minna sinks quietly toward the bottom.

Minna doesn't struggle at all.

Minna doesn't understand it herself.

Minna tells her mirror image, *Swim then, God damn it,* but

Minna doesn't swim.

———

The sun's shining.

Jette's placed the paper across her knee.

The paper's opened to the culture section.

The front page of the culture section is full of a woman.

The woman's Linda Lund.

Minna balances two cups of coffee.

Jette's busy smoothing out the paper.

Minna's having a hard time getting her legs to bend.

Minna glances at the mermaid's gaping gaze.

Minna glances at Linda.

Linda fills most of the front page.

Linda's shot with an out-of-focus lens.

Linda's mouth is slightly open.

Linda's eyes are deep and alert.

Linda sits and strokes her guitar.

The guitar no longer plays Segovia.

The guitar plays wistful pop.

People love wistful pop.

The guitar's positioned between Linda's legs.

People love Linda's legs.

Minna has goblins in her diaphragm.

Minna turns green.

Minna's terrible to photograph.

Minna's better in person, but

Linda looks lovely in the paper.

Minna can't breathe.

Minna's throat stings.

Jette rustles the paper excessively.

Jette lifts it up.

The paper's right in Minna's face.

Minna sees what Jette wants to show her:

Lars has written the article.

Lars has made the article fill seven columns.

Lars has used the word *sensual* in the headline.

Minna looks toward Christianshavn.

Jette knocks back her coffee.

Things are going well for Linda, Jette says.

Minna's tongue feels cold as bronze.

Minna's body starts shutting down.

The face chilly.

The heart pounding.

The larynx a clenched fist.

Nothing comes out.

Jette asks, *How's Lars, really?*

Minna's fingers tighten around her coffee.

Jette asks, *Do you still see each other?*

Minna has sat down but can't remain sitting.

Minna gets up and hops around a bit.

Minna has to pee.

Minna has to go to the john twice a day on average when
    she's at the Royal Library.

———

Minna wants to tell someone about her broken heart.

Minna feels pain in the solar plexus of her soul.

Minna needs a hot-water bottle.

Finn answers the phone.

Finn wants to chat.

Finn's a birdwatcher.

Finn's seen a bittern.

Finn knows where the nightingale lives.

Minna asks for Mom.

Mom comes to the phone.

Mom's glad to hear from her.

Minna's just about to cry, but

Mom and Finn have been to the Skaw.

Mom and Finn saw someone famous in a car.

Mom and Finn took a hike on Grenen.

The wind was blowing sand.

The sand got into everything.

Mom says that she misses Minna.

Mom feels like it's been a long time.

The clump in Minna's throat gets bigger.

The clump's a doorstop.

Minna can't say anything.

Mom goes quiet on the other end.

Mom and Minna are quiet together.

Minna whispers that she'll definitely come visit.

It won't be long, Minna says.

Mom says that of course they could come to Copenhagen.

Time's one thing we've got plenty of.

Minna doesn't like that Mom says *we*.

Minna says they'd be very welcome.

Minna says we should go to Copenhagen, Mom says.

Finn's indistinct in the background.

Mom laughs.

Mom tells her about the geraniums.

The geraniums are thriving in the east-facing windows.

The geraniums have an acrid scent in the sun.

The geraniums get photographed.

The geraniums get posted on the web.

Minna should go in and see.

Minna promises to look at Mom's blog.

Minna keeps her promise.

Mom's blog is kept rose pink.

Mom's blog is mostly photos, but

Text sneaks its way in between the geraniums.

Mom's written about her daughters on the blog.

The daughters live far away in Copenhagen.

The elder one's married to an optician.

The younger is unwed.

Mom isn't a grandma.

You can't get everything you wish for, Mom writes.

Minna stares at the text.

The text is more intimate than Mom's Christmas letter to
the family.

The text is more naked than Minna's seen Mom
in reality.

Nobody really reads it anyhow, Mom must've thought.

Somebody might read it by accident, Mom must've thought.

Both thoughts had appealed.

It started small.

It began as a lift of the skirt.

It took root gradually.

The web's become a diary for Mom.

Mom starts to versify.

Mom writes haiku.

Mom lets it all hang out.

The geraniums are pink and demure, but

Mom's stark naked.

Minna hastens to shut it off.

Minna considers calling up the Senior Club.

The Senior Club ought to explain the gravity to seniors.

The web's a jungle.

The jungle's full of monkeys.

Monkeys love the excrement of others.

———

Lars has had Linda on the front page.

Elisabeth's been in the Bookstore of the Unknown.

Jette sits on the quay.

Mom's on the web too often.

Dad's dead.

Lars has fur on his face, but

Lars's fur isn't quite like Minna's.

Minna's fur is a metaphor.

Lars's fur is real.

Minna's studied portraits.

Lars and Dad have a beard in common, but

Lars smelled of Aqua Velva.

Dad of salt.

Minna's looked at the map of Denmark.

Aarhus nestles in Marselisborg Forest.

Amager's on the other end of the country, or

Amager's in the middle of the country, or

Amager in any case is quiet for a brief moment.

The quiet makes room.

The quiet makes a dome over a moment's clarity.

The clarity lays bare a person.

The person is Minna herself.

Minna hasn't seen her own person for a long time.

Minna's person has split ends.

Minna's person has bags.

The person's hand trembles quietly.

The person's mouth hangs open.

Minna can hear a faint hum.

Minna thinks, *I used to sing* . . .

Minna gives herself the once-over.

Minna benefits from the examination.

Time now for a little holiday.

Other people aren't to join the holiday.

Minna hasn't been to Bornholm since she was fourteen.

Bornholm's almost Sweden.

Bornholm's in the opposite direction.

Bornholm's an island.

Bornholm's well suited to mental catharsis.

Lars will be forgotten.

The family'll have to take care of itself.

The family *can* take care of itself.

Minna orders a ticket to Ystad.

Minna wants to develop the ability to sort people.

Minna wants an asshole filter.

Minna no longer wants to be a host species.

Minna takes Bergman along.

Bergman can ride in the backpack.

———

Minna's sitting on the train to Ystad.

Minna's feeling chipper.

Minna's running away from it all.

Minna's breaking from the pack.

The pack is evil.

Minna doesn't want to be part of them.

Minna also feels melancholy.

Minna was sure it was something you grew out of.

Minna thought as a kid, *As soon as I grow up,* but

Grown-ups are kids who have lots to hide.

Dumb kids turn into dumb grown-ups.

Evil kids = evil grown-ups.

Minna gets the connection.

Minna walks around among ordinary people.

Ordinary people cheat on their taxes.

Ordinary people go to swinger clubs.

Ordinary people flee the scene of the crime.

Ordinary people enlist in the Nordland Regiment of the ss.

Ordinary people are quislings, collaborators, camp followers.

Ordinary people just need a stage.

The pig performs gladly.

Cowards are in good supply too.

Minna doesn't get how she could have ignored it.

Minna's clear-sighted enough.

Minna's watched tv.

Minna followed the war in the Balkans.

Minna watched neighbors out each other to Serbian militias.

One day you're tending cabbage together in the backyard.

The next you're on a bus headed for a mass grave.

Your best friend's a chameleon.

Evil's a state that can be conjured up.

Evil exists.

Minna supposes she's tarred with the same brush.

Karin isn't exactly without stain either.

Elisabeth is family.

Lars could've been.

Minna realizes that it's all about sorting.

Minna's got to judge people one at a time.

Minna wants to learn not to trust.

That's all going to be over now.

The last narcissist's gotten her to clap.

The last Jutlander's taken up residence in her in-box.

The last nymphomaniac.

The last reporter.

Indian demons.

Billy goats.

Kamikaze pilots.

Thieves in the night:

It's over!

Minna feels her backbone grow.

Minna's backbone sends out roots and shoots.

Minna's backbone blossoms.

Minna looks out upon the southern Swedish landscape.

The landscape drifts past like a fog.

Grown-ups are kids who become like animals, Minna thinks.

Minna tries dozing.

The train's got a school camp on board.

The school camp's blocked all exits.

The teacher screams that the school camp has to settle
   down a bit.

The teacher screams, SO SIT DOWN, FREDERIK!

The teacher screams, THERE ARE OTHER PEOPLE ON THE
   TRAIN!

That might be so, Minna thinks, but

Bergman's the only human on the train.

Bergman lies on her lap.

Dread makes the dreaded real.

That's true—or . . .

Minna listens to the school camp.

Minna dreaded *not* having a kid.

The school camp relieves the fear.

Kids are sweet, but

Kids reflect their parents' seamy side.

Bergman knows that.

Bergman had nine kids.

Bergman had to make films to get away from his kids.

Minna shouldn't be down in the mouth.

Anne Marie Carl-Nielsen is also along on the trip.

Anne Marie's along in Minna's mind.

Anne Marie preferred animals.

Anne Marie was into mermaids and horses.

Minna's more into cats, but

Minna will make do alone.

Minna's a composer!

Minna settles into her seat, thrilled about the ferry.

The Baltic is capricious.

The Baltic's deep and smooth.

The Baltic's a bowl, a submarine valley.

The Baltic's as balmy as a bathtub.

Minna's brought her bathing suit along.

It's late in August.

Minna's stoked.

Minna's heading away from what hurts.

No one's going to inflict any more damage, Minna thinks.
Everything's going to get sorted, Minna thinks, because
Minna wants to grow an asshole filter.
Minna thinks she can grow it quickly.
Minna's broken heart dwells in the breast of an optimist.

———

Minna's boarded the *Leonora Christine.*
The school camp's shepherded onto the upper deck.
The school camp's met another school camp.
The school camps exchange sexual fluids.
Minna drinks coffee in the stern canteen.
The canteen's full of retirees.
The retirees swarm up from the vehicle deck.
The retirees want to sit with one other.
Minna moves gladly.
Minna moves for two pairs of friends in their midseventies.
The gentlemen immediately order beer.
The missuses have newly permed hair.
The missuses make do with orange soda.
The gentlemen squeeze their permed missuses.
The missuses giggle.
The retirees have sex.
Minna can see they have sex.
Minna thinks of Mom.
Minna dismisses the thought.
The thought lands on Lars.
Lars without clothes on.

Lars with a hard-on.

Minna on horseback.

Cat on a hot tin roof.

Minna and Lars, genital to genital, no respect.

Minna blushes on the plastic ferry seat.

Minna's been the fuck buddy of a disrespectful man.

That's the way it is, thinks Minna.

Minna's backbone withers.

Lars prefers sex with a machete.

It's unbearable, but there you have it.

The retirees raise their glasses.

Minna takes up Bergman from her pack.

The *Leonora Christine* pulls away from the quay.

The *Leonora Christine* heads out.

Minna glances down at Bergman.

Bergman says, *I pretend to be an adult.*

Bergman says, *Time and again it amazes me that people take me seriously.*

Minna loves Bergman.

Bergman lunges for Minna with the truth.

Bergman holds her tight, and now she glances at the door to the vehicle deck.

The door opens.

A small group of retirees trickles in.

Minna feels initially serene at the sight.

It doesn't last.

Minna raises Bergman to her face.

Minna slouches in her seat.

Minna wants to get off the *Leonora Christine.*

The *Leonora Christine* has set course for Rønne, but

Minna wants to leave.

Minna was once a music teacher at a folk high school.

Minna taught weeklong classes for happy amateurs.

The happy amateurs signed up in torrents.

The folk high school provided housing.

The folk high school was always going bust.

The amateurs had dough.

People stood there with guitars and piccolos.

People wanted to be virtuous.

Minna tried to teach them a bit of notation.

Minna clapped in time.

Minna played Bach for them.

Minna was trampled by dwarfs.

Minna ran out of options.

Minna let them sing from the tired Danish songbook.

The amateurs sang, *Is the light only for the learnéd?*

Minna had her take on it.

The amateurs felt disgruntled about their rooms.

Minna found them new ones.

The amateurs lost their things:

Dentures, rollators, and spectacles vanishing every instant.

Prosthetic legs and large-print books: gone.

Grundtvig hovered above the waters.

Grundtvig illuminated the scene.

Grundtvig was high on sugar water and the life of the mind.

Minna had to see to all the practicalities herself.

The amateurs loved Minna.

The amateurs pinched her on the cheek.

The amateurs wanted to sing at the farewell party.

The party was full of music that Minna had inflicted on
their world.

Minna wept.

Minna felt ashamed.

Minna needed rent money.

Minna was keeping the wolf from the door, but

The wolf was preferable in the end.

Minna quit and is now en route to Bornholm.

Minna sits behind Bergman on the *Leonora Christine*.

Minna has recognized the hindmost retiree.

The retiree's named Gunvor Kramer.

Gunvor Kramer's a happy amateur.

Gunvor Kramer's a sincere person, but even worse:

Gunvor's on Facebook, and even worse:

Gunvor's convinced that she and Minna are colleagues.

Gunvor recorded a Christmas tape.

Gunvor recorded it on a reel-to-reel.

The reel-to-reel stands in Gunvor's living room.

Gunvor is thus a composer.

Gunvor writes Minna often.

Gunvor writes about her breakthroughs in the art of music,
but even worse:

Gunvor Kramer's aboard the *Leonora Christine*.

Gunvor Kramer's set a course for Minna.

Minna knows that her holiday hangs by a thread.

Gunvor's in a car, you see.

Gunvor would like to chauffeur Minna around the island.

Gunvor would like to sing all her compositions for
    Minna, vibrato.

Minna presses Bergman to her face.

Gunvor passes by somewhere to the rear.

Gunvor walks slowly, slowly.

Minna turns cautiously.

Gunvor has sat down two booths away, with her back
    to Minna.

It's silly of course.

Gunvor's merely a person.

Gunvor loves #544 in the tired Danish songbook.

Gunvor loves chain dancing.

Gunvor has a droopy bosom.

Minna was dragged in as an unwilling witness.

Minna tucks Bergman into her backpack.

Minna rediscovers her sunglasses.

The sunglasses slip down in front of her face.

Gunvor's started on the candy catalog.

Gunvor's found a ballpoint pen.

Gunvor sets checkmarks by candy.

The sunglasses shield Minna from Gunvor.

Minna passes Gunvor.

Minna's set a course for the stern.

Minna catches sight of the sea.

The Baltic lies blue and piercing.

The *Leonora Christine* shoves its way forward, self-confidence
  in its hull.
The *Leonora Christine* heads down the coast.
Minna slouches in a seat.
Minna hugs her backpack.
Minna oozes adrenaline.
Swedish customs opens for candy and liquor purchasers.
Swedish customs is full of retirees.
Gunvor forages.
Minna leans back.
No one heeds her anymore.
Minna's alone and can plan her escape.

———

Minna's arrived in Rønne.
Elisabeth's gotten ahold of her.
Mom's making plans for the weekend, but
Minna isn't home.
Elisabeth wants to know where she is, but
Minna's just not home.
Bornholm waits in the sunshine.
Bus #5 swoops across the island.
Minna's looking forward to seeing the landscape again.
Minna's quickly disappointed.
Bornholm had more cliffs in her memory.
Bornholm was exotic, Swedish.
Bornholm seems abandoned now.

The bus stop spots are dusty.

The butcher's closed.

The baker, the dairy, the school.

Bjarne's tanning salon has set up shop in the supermarket.

Bjarne's tanning salon browns the serfs.

Bjarne's tanning salon turns little girls into reality stars.

Bjarne makes a mint on the villages' decline.

The provinces assuage grief with porn.

The houses are cheap.

The houses have signs in their windows.

The houses are OPEN, OPEN, OPEN.

Most folks have fled.

Randiness remains.

Minna can see that a country's about to disappear.

Minna can see that the tracks point over the cliff edge.

Minna feels like a slum tourist.

That wasn't the idea behind my holiday, thinks Minna.

Minna regards a shelter in Østerlars.

The round church has decamped.

The round church has taken a room in Copenhagen.

Grief is latent in Minna.

Grief seizes its chance.

Minna gets moisture in her eyes.

Minna wipes the moisture away.

Minna wants to find a rock in the sea.

Minna wants to go out to the rock and sit.

Bergman will join her, and a thermos of coffee.

The cliffs begin someplace.

Minna googled Svaneke.

Minna saw the cliffs on the web.

The idyll will take over sooner or later.

Minna glances down in her backpack.

The cell phone sits down there.

Elisabeth's name throbs like an irate artery.

Minna shuts the pack.

Minna can see a large field of grain.

Minna can see a steep slope.

Bus #5 drives through the grain.

The sea appears at the foot of the hill.

The Baltic doubles over, vast and wet.

Bus #5 is headed toward Listed, and now it happens.

Bornholm opens up.

Bornholm looks like itself in the pictures.

The smokehouse has a flame under the herring.

Troll figurines have appeared in the windows.

The cliffs fall crumbling into the water.

The sea is blue-black, with swans in it.

The bus winds through charming houses.

The bus holds for a school camp.

The bus holds for another school camp.

The bus holds for a flock of retirees.

The bus swings gently down the coast and into Svaneke.

Minna presses the STOP button.

The bus stops by the hard-candy store.

Minna struggles with her wheeled suitcase, and then she's
        standing there.

Minna stands there and is reminded of the Old Town
    in Aarhus.

Minna's reminded of the trips to Ballehage Beach.

Minna remembers her toes on the pier.

Minna with webbed feet.

Minna with piano fingers.

Minna with song in her throat.

Minna with a future before her, but

Elisabeth rings loudly in the pack.

Elisabeth's on Minna's trail.

Minna refuses to yield.

Minna fumbles in her pocket for the address.

Minna's going to live in a room with a tea kitchen.

The room has a view over the harbor.

The landlady's a friend of a friend.

Minna is not hoping that the landlady's gregarious.

Minna wants to be alone in the Baltic.

Minna stands quietly on the square.

Minna sees people everywhere.

The people are speaking Copenhagen dialect.

The people are looking for a ceramist.

Minna stands in the people's way.

Minna must make way.

Minna wheels her suitcase forward and back.

Minna's in the midst of a transport tsunami.

———

The lodgings in this case are not lacking.

Half-timbering goes with everything.

The foundation is Bornholm granite.

The room has a table, sofa, and bed.

The room isn't missing a thing, *au contraire.*

The room has latticed windows with geraniums.

Minna's rubbed the scented leaves between her fingers.

Minna's said hello to the landlady.

The landlady was in her midforties.

The landlady bore the mark of tourism.

Minna said that she had to quote *work during her stay.*

Minna's used that trick before.

People with projects are left in peace.

Minna has one end of the house.

The door between Minna and the landlady is locked.

Nobody'll come barging in, the landlady assured her.

That's great, and yet it isn't anyway.

The landlady's got a dog.

The dog bays.

The dog's bayed ever since the landlady left to do
    her shopping.

Minna sees the dog before her:

The dog's muzzle pointed skyward.

The dog's lower lip pushed forward.

The dog's eyes squinting ceilingward.

The dog doesn't want to be alone.

Minna's just on the other side of the landlady's locked door.

The dog can hear Minna.

The dog doesn't understand that Minna can't rescue it.

Minna's hushed the dog through the keyhole.

Minna's acted as if she's gone to the grocery store.

The dog isn't fooled by cheap tricks.

The dog has nothing to do but complain about the program.

Minna puts her earplugs into action.

Minna sits in a soundproof bubble.

Minna can hear her breathing in the bubble.

Minna's lungs puff quietly.

Minna's pulse vibrates.

Minna closes her eyes and listens.

The ocean buzzes in Minna's veins.

The ocean calls from Minna's interior.

The ocean's outside the window, but

The ocean's inside Minna too.

Minna sits with the sea inside.

Minna ought to go for a walk, she knows.

Svaneke awaits outside and lovely.

People circle like good-natured sharks.

Minna should walk past them and out to a cliff, but

Minna's deaf and listens.

Minna's interior is a rehash of memories.

Minna paddles around in the old days.

Minna feels her body shifting.

Minna's senses are returning.

Hands down through the sand.

Hands up toward the gulls.

Dad's hand and Minna's.

The blue delta of Dad's hand.

The sea rises in Minna.

The sea finds fissures in Minna.

Minna's leaky.

Minna opens her eyes and blinks.

The sea trickles slowly.

The sea reaches land.

The beads of gravel rattle.

Minna blows her nose.

Minna should find herself a cliff.

Minna and Bergman should walk out onto the cliff and sit.

Minna shouldn't do anything else.

Minna feels like Gunvor's peeping in the window.

The geraniums block the inward view.

Bornholm's relatively large.

The likelihood's small, but

Minna peeks out from behind a plant.

Svaneke Harbor rocks with boats.

The tourists balance glass plates.

The tourists turn the corner in sensible shoes.

The tourists position themselves willingly in line.

The cliffs are out there.

The cliffs are warm from the day's sun.

Minna runs a hand across her face.

Minna opens her backpack.

Bergman's lying down there.

Dread makes the dreaded real, he repeats.

Minna nods.

Minna closes her eyes.

Minna whispers out into the lodgings: *Now the dog howls no more.*

The dog's done with playing forsaken.

The dog's shut its mouth.

The dog lies in its basket.

The dog begs for its ball.

The dog has nothing more to say about its situation.

Minna removes the earplug on the right side.

Minna listens with her head cocked.

—

The dog howls.

The dog howls skyward.

———

Minna's crawled out as far as she can go.

Minna sits on the blanket she brought.

The granite drills up gently into her buttock.

The gulls have set up camp on a couple cliffs farther out.

Christiansø is a seed on the horizon.

Christiansø beckons with its outpost nature.

Minna doesn't want to be any farther out now.

Minna just wants to sit here.

Minna wants to drink her coffee with Bergman.

The waves smack gently against the cliff.

The world smells of seaweed.

Minna sits and is doing fine.

Minna comes to think of Vagn.

Minna took a first-aid course of Vagn's.

Minna's never rescued anyone, but

Vagn knew all about hurt people.

Vagn said, *Hold their hand!*

Vagn said, *Bodily contact helps the injured!*

Vagn said, *Caresses and calm speech'll pass the time.*

The ambulance'll get there sooner or later.

A human being could use another human in the meantime.

A small hand is enough!

Minna looks around her circle of acquaintances.

The circle of acquaintances can't get a hand through
the shield.

The circle of acquaintances can't get skin on skin.

Minna considers her hand.

Minna doesn't need to play pious.

Minna's hand has withdrawn from the struggle.

Minna's hand hasn't touched anyone since Lars.

Lars was so real under the duvet.

Lars was so gentle down there.

Lars dared in the dark, but

The light demands trend awareness.

Minna's not trendy.

Minna's soft and warm every day.

The everyday doesn't cut it.

Minna takes her hand from the sea and sticks it in her
mouth.

The sea tastes good.

The lighthouse towers behind her.

Årsdale nestles to the south.

Christiansø is Denmark's remotest enclave.

This rock's a rehearsal space, thinks Minna.

The gulls are the only ones present.

Minna can make noise the way she wishes.

Minna feels something slipping far below.

Minna's belly grows in capacity.

The lungs become bellows.

The throat a swan's.

The voice full of rust.

Minna's needed rehearsal space, but

Bornholm's big.

Bornholm has no objection if Minna warbles a trill.

The song has light, Minna sings.

Minna doesn't know where it's coming from, but it persists.

The song has warmth, she sings.

Minna recalls the folk high school now.

The song has eternity.

Minna thinks it's a strange song.

Minna sings the song anyway.

Minna's voice rises plumb upward.

The voice is like a beanpole.

Minna can climb it.

Minna can reach the stars.

Minna can reach the giant, the golden eggs, the empyrean.

Minna's good at climbing, but then she dives.

It does the voice good to plunge headlong.

The voice breaks the surface of the sea.

The voice continues toward the bottom.

The sea grass sways and tickles.

The marine fauna stands still and listens.

The voice is alone with itself and the wet.

Minna closes her eyes and she sings,

The song unites as it fades.

That's not enough for Minna.

Minna gives the song a last burst.

Minna's heart lifts.

The gulls rise.

The wings flutter.

The wings applaud and applaud.

Minna opens her eyes, and there stands an angler.

The angler stands on the rock ten yards away.

The angler looks at Minna.

The angler creaks in his rubber boots.

The angler calls out,

The fish are getting spooked.

Minna blushes: *I thought I was alone.*

A kayaker instantly paddles past.

Another kayaker, and yet another.

The kayakers paddle past like geese in a village pond.

The angler points somewhere behind Minna.

Minna turns around.

The evening sun is blinding, but there sit a man and
    a woman.

The man and woman wave with their cigarettes.

The woman says it sounded lovely.

Minna repeats that she thought she was alone.

The woman and the man often sit by the lighthouse in the evening.

The view of Christiansø, says the man.

The view of the bathers, says the woman.

The woman points at a springboard a little ways off.

People are leaping from the springboard down among the cliffs.

Campground tents sprout up among the brush.

Minna doesn't want to know anything else, but

The couple's from Østerbro in Copenhagen.

The couple could stay on Bornholm forever.

The woman pinches the man on the thigh.

The man pinches the woman on the thigh.

The man has large lips.

The woman isn't wearing a bra.

Minna wishes it weren't embarrassing to leave.

Bergman smiles at her from down on the granite.

Bergman declares that she's never been lovelier, but

Bergman would lie worse than a horse runs if his prick were at risk.

Flight is a sign of weakness, she whispers.

Silence descends.

Silence is no longer a balm for the soul.

Silence is a social defect.

Minna feels the need to converse a bit.

Minna asks whether the couple has a cottage.

The woman says the cottage belongs to her husband.

The husband in question isn't along on holiday.

The man with the large lips on the other hand is along for the whole trip.

The man asks Minna where she's from.

Minna doesn't know what to say.

Minna has more of an impulse to cry.

Aarhus—, says Minna.

Minna is suddenly unsure.

Minna felt at home in the song a few minutes ago.

The song disappeared, down toward the bottom.

The song stands still among the herring.

Everything else belongs to another reality.

Everything else, Minna thinks to herself, *is mere geography.*

———

Minna's crawled into bed at her lodgings.

The landlady's not home.

The dog's inconsolable.

Minna's stuffed a quilt around the bottom of the door.

Minna's glad she has earplugs.

Minna's glad she's by herself again.

The man and woman wanted to accompany her to Svaneke.

Minna was dragged in as an unwilling witness.

Minna didn't escape the couple till they were at the harbor kiosk.

Disappointment inhabits her mind like rainy weather.

Minna really wants an asshole filter.

Minna wants to start setting boundaries.

Minna can't say either yes or no, and

Minna's legs feel heavy.

The duvet feels strange.

The lodgings smell of cottage.

Minna thinks of spooks.

Minna's only afraid of spooks once in a while.

Minna doesn't believe in spooks, but

Things you don't believe in often exist anyway.

The Grauballe Man haunted Minna one spring when she
    was a child.

The Grauballe Man lay dead in the Moesgård Museum, but

The Grauballe Man walks around at night.

The Grauballe Man wriggles out of his display.

The Grauballe Man stands out on the cobblestones.

The Grauballe Man walks into Marselisborg Forest.

The Grauballe Man loves nature—and Minna.

The bog man visits Minna at night.

Minna lies in her small bed with the duvet pulled up to
    her nose.

Minna lies and stares at the door of her room.

The living room resounds with the sound of coffee cups.

Elisabeth's room resounds with the sound of high
    school boys.

Minna lies with her eyes on stalks, and then!

The door opens, and who should enter?

Minna's friend from Marselisborg Forest.

The Grauballe Man smells of harness.

The Grauballe Man's body is a story of its own.

The head crushed.

The throat cut.

The feet flat and lumpy, but what's worse:

The bog man leans over Minna.

The bog man's picked anemones for Minna.

The bog man boasts of his earthly remains.

The bog man still has flesh on his bones.

Minna will end up a skeleton!

Dad too!

Mom!

Elisabeth?

Minna doesn't believe in spooks.

Minna believes in the Grauballe Man.

Minna lies in her Bornholm sanctuary.

Minna considers the spiritual probabilities.

Bergman haunts her too.

Elisabeth employs demons.

The Fenris wolf howls.

The spooks are coming if they exist.

Elisabeth's coming if she discovers where Minna is.

Elisabeth wants to have the little ones under her thumb.

Minna just wants to love the little ones.

Minna's little ones would never lack for sweets.

Minna's little ones would grow roly-poly.

Minna really can't say no.

It doesn't matter now anyhow.

Minna won't become anyone's mother, and

Kids are the worst spooks in the world.

Kids can't understand that they don't exist.

Kids stick their cold hands under the duvet.

Kids would like to slap the sleeper's face.

Minna collects herself.

Minna forces herself to think of dull things.

Minna makes plans for the morrow.

Minna wants to go farther out.

Minna wants to find a rock so desolate.

Minna wants to go out to the rock and sing.

Minna wants to make sure she's alone.

Minna wants to stand there and get everything to swing.

The song will vault higher and higher.

The sky will stretch itself open,

The waves cast themselves against the cliff,

The ships beat into the wind.

Minna presses herself down into her rented linen.

Minna pushes herself out of reality.

The children exit Minna's consciousness.

The children go with the Grauballe Man.

Marselisborg Forest closes up behind them.

The museum awaits.

The roe deer.

———

Minna's put on her bathing suit under her sundress.

Minna wants to go out and sing and get tan.

Minna wants to rock–bathe.

Minna has to get provisions first.

Minna's gone for a walk in town.

Svaneke's lovely.

Svaneke's light yellow.

Svaneke's a set piece, thinks Minna.

The sky a stage border.

The smokehouse a sort of canteen.

The knickknack shops = the costume department.

Minna plays with the motif, and there's something to it.

Minna does like Svaneke, but

Svaneke reminds her a bit of Linda.

The houses have tricked themselves out for the season.

The houses bulge with whitewashed plinths.

Minna raises her eyes to the horizon.

The ocean's not going anywhere.

The ocean's seen much worse.

The cliffs are above thoughts of time.

The Baltic! Årsdale!

Minna wants to hike toward Årsdale a bit later.

Minna wants to hike so far south that she can hike in peace.

Minna's looked at the map.

The rocks extend a long way out down there.

The rocks permit clambering.

Minna can walk far out onto the rocks.

Minna's on her way down and out, but

Svaneke Dairy is famed for its beer ice cream.

Svaneke Dairy lies en route.

Minna wants to have an ice cream to hike on.

The weather's good for ice cream, and lots of people have
    thought the same thing:
The tourists have formed a line.
The line reaches far out into the gravel.
The line hardly budges.
The small children crawl around on a plastic cow in
    the courtyard.
The mothers stand in line.
The fathers look after the kids.
The retirees rummage in their purses.
The retirees cannot find their spectacles.
The waitresses are dressed in Morten Korch costumes.
The waitresses resemble actresses from the fifties.
The waitresses look like Tove Maës and Ghita Nørby.
The waitresses hobble becomingly in their feudal shoes.
The waitresses look homespun by the latte machines.
Minna's crept forward a little ways in the line now.
Minna can see that there are celebrities in the line.
The celebrities take a long time to serve.
The retirees are on a first-name basis with the celebrities.
The small children ride the cow.
The fathers look at smartphones.
The mothers are ready to crack.
Minna on the other hand is of good cheer.
Minna wants to have a cup of coffee with her ice cream.
Minna's advanced far in the line.
Minna's about to order.
Tove Maës just can't see Minna.

Tove Maës can only see the celebrity.

The celebrity's from on TV.

The celebrity will have ice cream with licorice in it.

The celebrity will have espresso.

The celebrity flaunts the fact that he comes here often.

Tove Maës and the celebrity gossip about the locals.

Ghita Nørby limps out after more sherbet.

Ghita and Tove want most to serve the celebrity.

The celebrity can get what he wants.

Minna's been cut in front of twice now.

Minna raises her hand tentatively.

Minna gets up on tiptoe.

The celebrity laughs loud and long.

Tove Maës laughs loud and long.

The retirees' hip cement begins to crumble.

The kids will be confirmed soon.

The mothers and fathers have long since divorced.

Minna says, *Excuse me!*

Minna's surprised to hear her own voice.

Minna continues, *There are lots of folks who're waiting.*

Tove Maës freezes under her bonnet.

Ghita Nørby moves in frames.

Minna blushes with justice on her side.

Minna orders a caffe latte.

Minna orders a tub of beer ice cream.

Tove Maës hobbles over to the coffee machine.

Ghita Nørby shoots the celebrity a glance.

The celebrity walks out into the courtyard.

The retiree behind Minna smiles gratefully.

Minna looks proudly back at the line.

Minna regards the people she's rescued.

Minna's proud of her sudden asshole filter.

Minna sticks a feather in her cap.

Small victories count too, she thinks.

A hand pokes up in the middle of the line.

The hand pokes up and waves.

A large gray head pops to the side.

Gunvor's mouth is a gaping O.

Gunvor calls out Minna's name loudly in the dairy.

Minna! It's me! Gunvor Kramer! From the folk high school!

Minna hears her coffee fizz out of the coffee machine.

Tove Maës sends a wicked smile out of the corner of
her mouth.

Minna's asshole filter worked well two seconds ago, but
Minna's asshole filter has large holes in the mesh.

———

Gunvor Kramer's found a corner in the courtyard.

Gunvor Kramer's pushed Minna deep into the corner.

Gunvor Kramer's wearing a linen smock.

Gunvor Kramer's hair is pinned fast with a Viking clasp.

Gunvor's been thinking a lot about Minna.

Minna's made a big difference for Gunvor.

Gunvor was only capable of simple compositions.

Gunvor couldn't get larger works to hang together.

Gunvor mostly preferred music with a chorus.

Gunvor was stuck artistically.

Minna helped her advance.

Gunvor stands in the supermarket, and then it happens.

Gunvor has to run out of the store.

Gunvor has to go over to her car.

Gunvor seats herself behind the wheel.

Gunvor finds her notebook in her purse.

Gunvor writes down the lyrics.

Gunvor hums the melody.

This is just an example, says Gunvor.

Gunvor clears her throat.

Minna's coffee halts in front of her mouth.

The coffee steams in the morning heat.

The beer ice cream melts.

Gunvor sings a song.

The song's about love.

Love is vulnerable, sings Gunvor.

Love falls to pieces so easily, she sings.

People are so busy.

No one should forget anybody.

No one should forget anybody.

Gunvor's eyes are large and shiny.

Gunvor's finished now.

Gunvor says that it's the prologue to a cantata.

The cantata's still missing a lot.

Minna smiles and grasps her beer ice cream.

Minna moves over on the bench.

Minna says, *It's good to know you got something out of the class.*

Gunvor scrapes the bottom of her sherbet tub.

Gunvor asks how long Minna's going to be on Bornholm.

Minna answers vaguely.

Gunvor gets an idea.

Gunvor's planned a day trip to Dueodde.

It's hot, Gunvor says, *let's go down and bathe.*

Minna says, *I'm not big on swimming.*

Gunvor points at her sundress and asks, *Why the bathing suit?*

Minna needn't reply.

Minna doesn't owe Gunvor a reply.

Gunvor's already moved on anyhow.

Gunvor tells her about the sand in Dueodde.

The sand is fine.

The sand gets into every fold of skin.

Gunvor slaps her thighs.

The skinfolds quiver.

Something moves inside the linen smock.

Minna feels powerless, especially in her face.

Minna needs to put up a fight.

Minna's mouth tries to come up with a lie.

Minna's mouth doesn't want to say anything.

Gunvor's mouth doesn't want anything but, but now Minna
  gets lucky:

The backpack rings.

Minna's backpack is sitting on the bench and ringing.

Gunvor looks at the backpack.

Minna knows quite well who's hiding in the pack.

Minna opens it up anyway.

People ought to go away when they talk on their cells.

Anything else is rude.

Minna presses the answer button.

Minna gets up carefully from the bench.

Minna leaves the corner with Gunvor.

Minna here.

It's about time! says Elisabeth.

Elisabeth gets down to business.

Elisabeth's been saving up.

Minna walks hesitantly through the courtyard.

Minna approaches the cow.

Elisabeth pricks up her ears on the other end.

Elisabeth asks, *Who are those kids?*

Minna says, *I don't know.*

That's true enough, but not true enough for the sister.

Elisabeth says that it's hard to be related to Minna.

Elisabeth says that it's getting harder and harder.

Elisabeth says that Mom and Finn are coming for
    the weekend.

Mom and Finn can't stay in Potato Row.

The bench isn't for sitting on, she says.

Elisabeth says, *If Minna went to Aarhus more often.*

Elisabeth says that it'd never happen if . . .

Minna's rounded the corner of the dairy.

Svaneke Harbor lies before her.

The boats rock in the late-summer breeze.

Gunvor sits in the courtyard.

Minna has her backpack with her.

Minna's sandals have nonslip soles.

Nothing's to prevent her.

The path is clear.

Who's going to stop her?

The sister wants to know where Minna is, and

Minna's running.

Minna's running down to the harbor.

Minna's on her way south, away from Svaneke.

Elisabeth says, *Answer me! Where?*

Minna says, *I'm on my way to Årsdale.*

Elisabeth doesn't know where Årsdale is.

Årsdale's in North Jutland, Minna says.

Årsdale's a little place south of Aalborg.

Everybody knows that, Minna says.

Minna can hear that Elisabeth didn't know that.

Minna can hear her sister's disbelief, but

Minna's positive, and now the connection's breaking up.

The connection crackles and hisses.

The connection gets so bad that Minna disappears.

Minna disappears.

Minna's feet take wing.

Minna's an instance of female buoyancy and helium.

———

The rock's flat and sloping.

The rock's wet at the base.

The sun hangs heavy as a plum.

The sea's blue–black.

Minna's observed:

The Bay of Aarhus is a fresh blue plain.

The Sound's a bottle-green river, but

The Baltic's black and greasy.

Minna's taken off her sundress.

Minna's smeared herself with SPF 20.

Minna stands with her toes so that they get wet.

Minna wants to rock-bathe, but

The sea grass waves under the surface.

The bladder wrack has lashed itself fast.

The rock looks like a woman's sex under the surface.

Minna isn't really sure and glances behind her.

Minna had to clamber to get here.

Minna had to crawl and injure herself.

Minna had to rest en route.

Minna was in flight of course, but

Minna isn't thinking about Gunvor anymore.

Minna stares at the sea.

Minna sees the darkness shift downward.

The darkness is deep on deep.

The loneliness profound.

Minna's got plenty of time.

Minna doesn't have to throw herself in.

The sky's vaulting.

The clouds assume their positions.

Minna's belly swells.

Something trickles.

Something else slides.

Minna lays her hands upon her midriff.

Minna inhales deep into her lungs.

Minna tilts back her neck.

Minna makes her mouth round, and then it arrives:

Minna sings a song in Latin.

Minna sings it with all that should've been.

Minna doesn't pull her punches:

Sed eligo quod video

Collum iugo prebeo;

Ad iugum tamen

Suave suave transeo.

The song feels like an incantation.

Latin has a menacing effect.

The words are like holy water.

The pelvis swaying.

The arms floating.

The feet stomping.

Minna chanting.

The sea licking her toes.

The song begins anew.

The song presses its way out again and again.

Minna senses the water's presence at her feet.

Minna thinks it's just grand getting cold feet.

Minna raises her voice as loud as it'll go.

The voice'll go very loud.

The voice can go maybe just loud enough too.

Minna wants to take a step backward.

The rock's slippery.

Minna's foot slips.

Minna slips with it.

Minna's legs rail against the sky.

Minna's head plunges toward stone.

Minna lands badly on her skull.

The skull breaks the fall of an entire woman.

Minna slides down into the water.

Minna slides down through the seaweed.

Minna sinks like a stone.

Minna's arms plow the water.

Minna's eyes are open and alive.

Minna's mouth is moist and round.

The sea feels like sweet chill.

The Baltic is a bowl.

The Baltic's a submarine valley.

Beauty won't deny itself.

The fish scoot off in gleaming procession.

The fish turn and pivot for Minna.

The scales glitter.

The eyes shine silver.

Minna reverts downward.

Minna wriggles her arms.

Minna waves to the darkness.

The darkness waves back.

Minna sees a gestalt in the darkness.

The gestalt has a beard.

The gestalt's mouth is a soft wet brushstroke.

Chest hair forces its way upward.

The beard wanders downward away from its chin.

An Adam's apple lies in the middle of the hair.

Dad? Minna thinks.

Dad waves.

Dad takes hold of Minna.

The fauna closes around them.

Bubbles seep from nose and mouth.

Hair flutters like sea grass.

Minna's pelvis has never been so round.

Minna's legs fuse and articulate.

Dad smiles at Minna.

Dad swims around Minna.

Minna says, *Helgenæs?*

Minna gets water in her mouth.

Minna gets a lot of water in her mouth.

Minna's lungs squeeze.

The lungs stretch.

The lungs are hard as cement.

The lungs don't want anything but to go upward.

Minna could happily continue downward, but

Minna's lungs want to go up.

Minna's bruised skull like a cork.

Minna's skull directional.

Minna's arms wretched fins.

Minna's legs kick and thrash.

The legs strike bedrock.

Minna's hands strike granite.

The rocks close around Minna.

Minna grasps the seaweed strands.

Minna grabs hold of Bornholm from below.

Minna throws up her arms in late-summerness.

Minna scrabbles on stone.

Minna searches for a chink.

Minna contracts like a muscle before it explodes.

Minna clings to dry land, angry and insecure.

Minna's tongue feels cold as bronze.

The sun acting up.

The corneas drying out.

Minna hauls herself farther up, and then she lies there.

Minna has rock-bathed.

Minna's been down and out.

Minna's toes plash in the surface of the ocean.

The rest of Minna has been decently salvaged.

Minna's world stands still.

Minna thinks of Dad in the water.

Minna thinks of her head.

Minna's head was apparently injured a bit.

The head hurting.

The mouth spitting.

Snot running.

The sun and the gulls having a look-see.

Minna lies with eyes shut.

Minna lies and listens.

Something rustles.

Minna raises her eyes, and there stand a pair of rubber shoes.

The shoes sit on a pair of feet.

The shoes shuffle uncertainly.

Hair pokes well out from the ankles.

A man has come to Minna's rescue.

Minna can't be bothered.

Minna's not going to be rescued now.

Minna's rescued herself.

Minna props herself up on an elbow: *Yes?*

The man asks, *Are you okay?*

Minna says, *I've been in the water.*

The man hunkers down: *On purpose?*

Minna says, *Not completely.*

The man wants to know if he should call for an ambulance.

Minna places her hands on the rock.

Minna raises herself a bit to sit.

Minna can see the man better now.

The man's plump.

The man has a beard.

Medium height.

The face attractive, and the mouth now opening.

The man says he could hear someone singing.

The man says he crawled out to have a look.

The man's got a banjo on his back.

Minna points at the banjo.

The man looks at the banjo as if it weren't his.

The banjo's his.

The banjo and he were on their way to Årsdale.

The man plays banjo during the tourist season.

Guitar's more for the mainland.

The man introduces himself.

The man says his name's Tim.

Tim seats himself at Minna's side.

Tim sets the banjo up against Minna's backpack.

Tim takes hold of Minna's hand.

Minna's hand is wet and cold.

Tim squeezes the hand a little.

The ambulance isn't out of the picture.

The medicopter isn't either.

Tim raises his index finger.

Tim says Minna should follow it with her eyes.

Tim's finger oscillates, but

Minna has her eye on something else.

The penny's dropped:

Tim's on Bornholm.

Tim's the cousin.

Tim knows someone with a rehearsal space in Kastrup.

The rehearsal space is cheap.

Minna can't stop looking.

Tim's family resemblance seeps out.

Tim does look like Lars.

Tim's beard is just more modest.

Tim also looks gentler.

Tim seems nice.

Tim's just about sweet.

Tim is Lars, like Lars was at night.

Tim is Lars without deadlines and Linda.

Lars was a porcupine.

Lars was a pillbox.

Tim's warm and hairy.

Tim's soft and shy.

Tim looks at her worriedly.

Tim says that she's bleeding from her head.

Minna says, *Who isn't?*

Tim says she's freezing, but

Minna isn't freezing.

It was me who sang, says Minna

    and then she shoots, she shoots him the mermaid eye.

Days

1. *So much for that winter,*
2. I thought, looking at the last crocuses of spring;
3. they lay down on the ground
4. and I was in doubt.
5. Chewed out an entire school because a single sentence bugged me
6. and drank my hot chocolate, *sweet/bitter.*
7. Worked,
8. considered traveling somewhere I never imagined I'd find myself
9. yet stayed where I was
10. and banged on my neighbor's wall,
11. was in doubt, but sure,
12. was insecure,
13. stood still by the window,
14. let my gaze move from running shoes to wool socks
15. and lay down on the bed.

1. Was attacked by a cross between a Rottweiler and a Great Dane in Søndermarken, survived.

2. Yelled at five dog owners in down jackets, *YOU'RE ALL SICK!*

3. Survived.

4. Ran my route (cemetery, Frederiksberg Gardens, Søndermarken, home) faster than ever.

5. Propped my hands on my knees and howled at the floor,

6. *Why this now too? Hasn't it been enough? Hasn't it?*

7. I howled

8. and found I'd sustained injury from dog attack on the left side of my tongue,

9. but surviving, *always surviving,*

10. that's the way I am, *not the kind you can knock out,*

11. with tongue before the mirror,

12. eyes open,

13. my face a grimace of gums and longing

14. and ice water for dinner.

1. Pondered what it meant to be happy.
2. Decided to test what would happen if I were happy,
3. *really happy.*
4. Was afraid to be disappointed.
5. Cleaned the fridge,
6. thought about what he'd written
7. and kept returning to the word *self-confidence,* wrote that down too,
8. wrote it down again
9. and went to the supermarket.
10. Took in the bottle of wine the neighbor had placed on my mat:
11. *Excuse the noise, Love, Majbritt,* it said; *so that's her name, I thought,*
12. and set the bottle atop the fridge,
13. moved it under the sink,
14. I'll drink it for Pentecost,
15. for Pentecost when I'm happy,
16. really happy.

1. Woke at the sound of my mirror falling down, *and that cannot be good.*

2. Salvaged the glass, but had to go down to the backyard with the frame, *and that cannot be good.*

3. Considered crawling under the blankets

4. or going on a bike ride

5. or making a change—*gills, paws, antennae*—

6. but could not.

7. Ascertained that when the wind's in the east, Valby's Siberia,

8. roughly just as empty

9. and full of loose dogs running from hedge to hedge, no doubt after dead birds.

10. Went for an evening walk on Queen Dagmar's Boulevard.

11. Heard kids practicing the flute through half-open windows

12. while blackbirds up on the chimneys sang to themselves

13. and to the dogs by the hedges

14. and me on the street beneath Langgade Station.

1. Woke an hour early,

2. made instant coffee,

3. drank it,

4. stood by my kitchen window the same way I stood by my kitchen window when I lived on the island of Fanø and went down to the beach every day and crushed razor shells underfoot: *Why do I live here?* I'd wondered

5. and couldn't have known that one day I would stand in a flat in Valby and look at the crooked tulips in the backyard and wonder the same thing.

6. Wrote.

7. Went for a walk in the cemetery, where everything promises spring, and stopped, as I often do, by Vilhelm Kyhn's grave, and Kyhn would always stay the same, rendered in bronze and grown into the birch tree that gnarls above him,

8. *one day I'm going to have to take a picture of that tree,*

9. *one day it'll be something I can show from time past,*

10. I resolved and pilfered a twig,

11. watched the news,

12. watched my face go past in the hallway,

13. watched my feet in woolen socks far below

14. crushing nothing.

1. Hard wind from the east and everything smelled of southern Sweden.

2. Tidied up my bulletin board,

3. went for a run through Søndermarken and through the cemeteries, for now it is spring, *and it's tough to be happy on schedule, and rarely does anyone get what they deserve,* yet now it is spring.

4. Took notes that later might prove useful, *and everything's dicey, but quiet.*

5. Thought of the people you're allowed to like, the ones you're not allowed to, and the ones you really do anyway *but never mention a word about.*

6. Gave my secrets a good going-over,

7. *and I haven't given up hope, I still believe that things can open and become soft and alive, German bunkers, Berlin walls, abandoned abattoirs, it's only a question of time and it's all well in the end,* I thought in line at the grocer's

8. and stopped then on the way home outside Blankavej #25, first floor, where someone has a Mao figure standing on the windowsill and when I walk past, I sometimes think he waves and smiles, while other times it looks as if he gives me the finger,

9. it depends on my belief in things, *and if it were always positive, I'd be crazy,* I thought,

10. pleading with myself to raise my head, *maybe it wasn't at all his intention to make it sound that way,*

11. so forget it,

12. forget the view that day across the canal,

13. forget the winter-gray roofs,

14. the way the mitten got snagged on the banister,

15. the hoarfrost and the sort of things that remain,
16. shrug it off, forget it,
17. the injustice of it all,
18. for now it is spring.

1. That which was yesterday in bud, today is in bloom: the carnations on my table,

2. the territorial blackbird on the roof, the faint grumbling from my mouth and fridge.

3. *To reconcile yourself,* I thought,

4. and shrugged it off

5. and put on the Brahms again.

6. Thought about the art of loving,

7. about the art of loving in the right way, the art of loving casually, the art of not loving when you love, the art of loving even though you can't, the art of ceasing to love what you cannot help loving, the art of loving even though it doesn't pay, and waiting, the art of waiting,

8. and then I went down to the street and glanced to either side,

9. no dogs, no cars, just a couple people in the rain

10. and me.

11. Bought an ice cream cone,

12. walked around with it slightly raised before me,

13. got wet but didn't care, *for people who don't know how I feel should stop feeling for me, and if they can't think my thoughts to their conclusion, they should think about something else, maybe they should think about their own lives, and when they think about them, they should ask themselves if their lives make more sense*

14. *and do they?* I wondered

15. and walked home to Brahms

16. and the sounds down in the street.

1. Awoke, walked barefoot across the floor

2. and ate a bit of bread,

3. took a scrap of paper from the desk and wrote *A red elephant is still an elephant* on it

4. and grew anxious about whether that sort of thing was good enough, felt stupid, felt wan, was myself like an elephant that lurches around and knocks things over, *but an elephant among broken glass is still an elephant, just as a person who isn't up to snuff is still a person, and the Brooklyn movie theater is still a movie theater, and the grieving heart is still a heart, and a red elephant is still an elephant.*

5. Took the bike to Damhus Pond, and it was when I had to brake by the bird-feeding area that I thought of my taxes

6. and then my accountant,

7. and then I biked home to my receipts,

8. crunched the numbers,

9. and *This is a condition,* I wrote at the bottom of a heating bill,

10. *this is a way of being,*

11. *a change in the structure of existence*

12. like the lull of rainy Sunday mornings,

13. like trampled sneakers and slightly sour cartons of cream,

14. and birds on the ground that eat from your hand and shit in place rather than flying,

15. and birds ought to fly,

16. a bird that doesn't fly is no longer a bird.

1. Said thanks but no thanks to a matinée at the opera,

2. sat instead in the heat as it bit by bit filtered down from the drying attic to the fifth floor,

3. but Western Cemetery is Denmark's largest burial ground for the dead, so the living such as I can sunbathe without being seen by anyone but the collared doves on the small plot of land north of the willow allée, *and I'm not saying where.*

4. Took off my sandals, and my jersey,

5. got freckles,

6. got an urge to bike through South Harbor into the city and hike around the lakes, hadn't done that since New Year's Day, which was when he wrote,

7. *I keep imagining how much it must've hurt to shoot yourself in the heart with such a big rocket flare.*

8. Stood still on Queen Louise's Bridge to write down what the old man said as he squeezed his way between a young couple: *Just set it down in F major,* he said, and went on toward Nørrebro,

9. and January feels so far away on a day like this, when the clouds form over Sortedam Dossering, and kids with bike helmets wobble along the bike paths while they call to the fathers who have stuck broomsticks in through the back of their bikes so they don't fall,

10. *but the soul has a long time horizon.*

11. Biked home and made coffee in my Moka Express

12. and drank it, squeezed out the dishrags, picked candle wax off the table, *and I'm bad at being grumpy, but I have stamina, and I'm good at remembering and at loving and forgetting*

13. To be seen as a person amid the January dark

14. that is no more.

1. Slept as if someone shook me to see if I were awake.

2. Went to the pharmacy, where the woman with globular breasts took all the headache pill variants down and explained the differences, and her breasts get bigger and bigger every time I go, because she wants to tell me what camphor does to mucous membranes even though I'm buying earplugs, and I have to look at the inhaler even though I'm asking for Band-Aids, and I'm certain that these breasts the size of floating dry docks started out as ping-pong balls before behavior made them grow.

3. Walked home slowly,

4. lay on the bed

5. and let an hour's sleep turn into three, entangled in the bedspread like a swaddled babe,

6. woke, put my socks in the drawer,

7. told myself the story of when I met the crown prince, again and again,

8. told it so many times that it got pathetic, whereupon several wounds sprung leaks.

9. Made pasta Bolognese

10. and went for a walk through a world that to rub salt in my wounds had turned itself the wrong side out and revealed all its inner beauty,

11. all that fertility in the air, all that weeping in wait, and I'd taken the long way just to see if the elephants in Frederiksberg Gardens had lain down for the night, and the only ones left were the wood pigeons who sat in the grass.

12. *It might have been otherwise,* I thought, and looked up at the door that now and then stood ajar to the world, sometimes merely so it could poke its fingers in my face,

13. and yet

14. other times I catch a glimpse within as of a whale
    rising up from the sea with its tiny good clear eye
    peering at me, infinitely mild and inquiring after its
    long journey from the bottom, *Are you okay?*

15. *Not completely, no, for all that I originally asked for was*
    a cup of coffee

16. and now look at all this.

1. Ran around Damhus Pond, with all the ducklings shunted out of the way in the grass.

2. Ran so slowly that I was caught by a father and his little boy, and *Are there sharks in that water, Dad?* the boy asked, and the father replied, *Might be,*

3. and if he'd looked back he'd have seen me nod.

4. Couldn't sit inside for the sun, couldn't avoid Frederiksberg Gardens, but there weren't any elephants, only their smell.

5. Drew a line in the gravel with my sneakers.

6. Sat on a bench by the goldfish pond in the graveyard,

7. opened my bag and sat like that: me and my notes and an ice cream from the cross-eyed man in the kiosk, and yet there lay everything I ought to be observing with the shiny side up.

8. *I don't know if it's worth it,* I thought,

9. *I think that'll do now,*

10. and then I nodded to the old gaffer who was talking to himself on the bench opposite, and he might have had Alzheimer's, or perhaps he was about to make notes too, for he nodded back,

11. and he was mournful, but alive and kicking,

12. and *We should have the courage to keep at it,* he whispered. *We should believe, lose, love, be lost and again found,*

13. and he looked at me, whispering,

14. *Necessity is the only criterion,*

15. and he whispered, *Forget the pillories,*

16. whispered, *Have patience and confidence till the end,*

17. and then I took out my pencil,

18. and it's possible I imagined it

19. but I was sure he giggled.

1. Caught sight of something so small that I couldn't really see it and longed for it to be larger,

2. *such a little window into such a big greenhouse.*

3. Had to sit on the edge of a kitchen chair and push away the newspaper,

4. *but breathing is a triangle with the point at the bottom and I'm on top, and if I hold my breath long enough my arms will turn into wings.*

5. Ran my fingertip along the edge of an iris, there where it curls inward, and then tugged up the zipper to the darkness *(that's allowed)*

6. and bought white flowers for forty crowns.

7. Leafed through a book.

8. Watched one pigeon mount another on the chimney across the backyard, whereupon they went their respective ways along the ridge, balancing, totally matter-of-fact, *while those of us over here in our segment know that nothing done is undone,*

9. and that you have to take the consequence.

10. Agreed with myself never to wear a large hat, not even if I could use some class,

11. *necessity,* I thought, *alone* and stuck my foot out into the crosswalk on Roskildevej.

12. Walked down the long paths, past Vilhelm Kyhn

13. and home again

14. to the flat and my relation to myself. It's always dicey,

15. you never know what awaits—an accident, a counterattack, another's joy, or simply a thought, like when I sat in Chinatown and ate Peking duck and a revelation ran through my head at a point when I couldn't listen: *Pull yourself together, little girl, this sort of thing doesn't happen in real life.*

16. Chopped lettuce without cutting my finger

17. and decided that perhaps in time something good would happen. I do know that something will, I know it, like when you're riding a train across Zealand in winter:

18. darkness darkness darkness darkness

19. and then suddenly a greenhouse crackling warm

20. in the middle of it all.

1. Woke slowly to the scent of wet sky.

2. Couldn't think of a better way to start the day than to run around in the rain in a cemetery,

3. transcribed straight from a gravestone onto my moist palm the name of Anna Mess *(and without reality we'd have lost the knack of fiction long ago).*

4. Wondered why I'm always thinking about Refshale Island, and came to no conclusion,

5. *but when I was young, we'd go to the air show once a year, and there was a place where kids were allowed to sit in the cockpit of a Draken, and the pilot lifted kid after kid up into the plane, first one boy and then another, and then he looked at me standing next to my mom.* I suppose you're going to try to fly too? *But I wouldn't, for what if the sky's a far better place, I thought, clinging to my mom's leg,*

6. and seen from that perspective, love is what binds us to the earth.

7. Got caught in a thunderstorm by Valby PO.

8. Got caught in a hail shower under the awning of Café Sommerfuglen.

9. Got caught in a downpour at the library, in a side wind, in the constant dripping from the leaky gutters on Horsekildevej

10. and kept standing there anyway

11. until I walked through the graves and the magnolia trees home.

1. It'll end well, this business. It'll end well. It almost can't help but. Denmark's too tiny and there will always be doors I'll find myself entering, and then we'll stand there face to face, me and his rap sheet,

2. *and we'll be able to have a conversation,* I thought,

3. *it doesn't make sense otherwise,* I thought,

4. and seated myself in the graveyard among daisies and dandelions, and

5. *it's tough now, yes, right now it's like driving a car in quicksand and suddenly realizing that the answer lies in the glove box, but you can't reach the glove box, the glove box is two inches beyond your reach, your fingertips are tingling in the air but the glove box is out of reach and it's in there, the wig, the magic potion, the pardon.*

6. But it'll end well, I thought, looking at the daisies.

7. My birthday was in fifteen days (nearly midlife), but it'll end well, my life. With patience, industry, and goodwill, it'll end well.

8. Biked into town and sat in a café near Kastellet.

9. Went when the shadows fell, round and round the fort, down to the water, as I usually do, through Nyhavn, as far as I could with arms swinging and the wind in my face, back to the Nyboder quarter, where I put on my bike helmet

10. (and it'll all work out fine).

11. Ate ramen while I gazed down at the pigeons in the backyard, *and I'm not stupid, and I'm not blind either,* I thought,

12. so it'll end well. I know that. It cannot anything but. It ends with my fingers stretching farther and farther and reaching all the way to the glove box without being able to reach it anyhow, but just when my nails are

almost able to scratch at the laminated vinyl it opens anyway, the glove box, it opens of its own accord, it opens, for that is what it was made for and wants to do, and the light goes on and there it lies within:

13. the pardon.

1. Found a picture of the bench in Manhattan where
   I once sat eating my fruit and writing my postcards:
   Hey everybody, the world's exactly like it is back home

2. (but it wasn't).

3. My mouth hurt,

4. I was dizzy

5. and found a spot to lie in the sun:

6. boxwood, lilacs, some obelisks, and among the stiffened
   pigeons a magpie that looked at me with its impudent
   head aslant, and I'm sure it had its eye on my sandals.

7. Listened to the unoiled rollator wheels of the widows
   passing by.

8. Saw a heron soaring high above, round and round, and
   from a distance it resembled both poultry shears and one
   of those scavengers.

9. *And have I ever been in the us?* I asked myself

10. while I looked at my hands

11. and walked over to the elephants,

12. found a bench, dug out a little water and my apple
    and observed that elephants can be a bit unsteady on
    their feet too, not to say dizzy, *and I am dizzy, as if
    there's someone who's calling me up without using a phone,
    and I don't know where my receiver's located, but when
    I close my eyes all sorts of things are streaming toward me.*

13. Made a note to myself: there's the reality that the others
    keep an eye on, and next to it is my own.

14. Took a detour home

15. and maybe it's the heat, maybe it's bloat or dehydration
    or some sort of blessing,

16. but in any case I'm dizzy.

1. Woke up dizzy.

2. Went sweatily around my flat beneath the drying attic, and water didn't seem to help.

3. Tucked the papers in my bag,

4. seated myself somewhere near the Round Tower and its observatory,

5. seated myself with my minor infections invisible to the naked eye, suddenly caught in the sunshine, and I thought, *So the time has come to learn to surrender.*

6. Walked in the afternoon's warmest hour down the main pedestrian drag and into a bookstore, to caress one maybe two books on the spine, *because that's why they stand there, they're just like the rest of us, they want to be caressed and loved despite it all,*

7. I thought, and saw there was a figure from TV, balancing with an ice cream cone outside the window on a miniature bike.

8. Embarked for home, scalding hot, like a little steel espresso pot,

9. lay down, thought, *There's nothing wrong with me, but if I lie still then the echo chamber might stop tormenting me,*

10. but it didn't.

11. Dozed, took a stroll as slowly as I could, elastic as a dromedary, languid and lazy amid nature's example for emulation: *Come on, just overdo it,*

12. and everything so lovely that it trembles, and I stand, undeterrably dizzy in the midst of it all

13. and listen, now the blackbird's singing

14. and soon the chestnut will blossom.

1. Opened my hand and grabbed hold: *I'm not letting go.*

2. Set the fan four inches from the table.

3. Went for a walk in Western Cemetery,

4. sat in the shade of a dawn redwood and gazed at the monument of some random industry baron, pyramidal and ivied and all, and I thought,

5. *He's just like an Indian, that's what he is, an Indian who enters his teepee after the lost battle to find the Indian in himself. He sharpens his spear, confronts his demons, sings about the night, sticks cords through his chest muscles and hoists himself through pain toward the light. He does it to find the Indian in himself again, and when he's discovered him, he steps out of the teepee. And his woman is a squaw who's seen the Indian in him the whole time and, no matter what he does, is able to see the Indian in him, but she also knows that the man she loves is precisely the sort of Indian who, after the lost battle, enters his teepee to find the Indian in himself again, so she doesn't go anywhere. Where should she go?*

6. Sat out in the sun,

7. lay down to read but looked chiefly at the sky, full of hoverflies and planes, and I'm not going anywhere. Where should I go?

8. Scribbled down an inscription: IN GRATITUDE.

9. Scribbled down an inscription: ALWAYS MISSED

10. and thought, *No doubt it's just a transition phase,*

11. and then I walked home,

12. clipped my nails,

13. and drank my coffee scalding from the pot while I looked at my hand holding the nail clippers, the pen, and the memory of things I have seen and held true,

14. and it held on, my hand, *it's not letting go.*

15. How could it?

1. Woke and could tell that it'd be a good day.

2. Biked to Dragør, which was the spit and image of the village I lived in on the island of Fanø.

3. Walked the bike straight out to the Sound and looked out toward Sweden, where clouds were gathering, but it didn't matter, *because above me the sky is always blue.*

4. Read, in the scent of saltwater, wet dogs, and children, until the mist reached the Øresund Bridge,

5. bought a shawl in a dime store

6. and ate an ice cream cone on the lawn in front of one of the cannons that in 1808 had sent seventy balls into the hull of the *Africa,* pride of the British fleet, *and 'twas on a day like this, with jam in the corners of the mouth and the will to believe that the tide of battle had turned.*

7. Walked along the water,

8. sat down by the harbor,

9. gazed at the swans while a father and his little boy raced along the breakwater, on a day with no trapdoors but with swans and the breeze on my face, *and there is peace, there is only kindness and good intentions and abundance in the hollyhocks, the half-timbering and the swans, the swans and then all the saltwater below.*

10. Biked homeward and was already freezing in my summer frock by the white church in Dragør.

11. Biked through the airport tunnel just as a Boeing or something took off, and the pressure and its flight out into the world shook the ground, the bike, and me as I sang, because no one would be able to hear me anyway in all the happiness

12. of just such a blind and sated Pentecost Copenhagen.

1. It was the sky from the morning,

2. the sky and my hand resting on the duvet,

3. and it was the rain and the writing on the wall, on the shopping list, in the letters

4. and the walk in the cemetery under white hawthorn, red hawthorn, and me and a squirrel in the willow allée.

5. Reserved a table at the hotel for me and Dad and Mom, *and I'm looking forward to them seeing where I live, and I'll show Dad the planetarium and Christiansborg Palace, and I'll show Mom that that house by the Søndermarken streetcar stop where she once lodged for a week as a twenty-year-old, not knowing that one day her children would exist and that her daughter would stand brimming and point, that that house is still standing.*

6. Thought about my dentist while I boiled eggs,

7. wrote a crucial note,

8. had an attack of vulnerability from the silence that fights back

9. and then took a walk on Queen Dagmar's Boulevard among the girls hopscotching and the boys with their scooters and then me and my insecurity, *but the one who writes must dare to stand with her fledglings stuck to her fingers and surrender them in showers of spittle and roses*

10. and keep going, because it's important

11. and keep going, because it's alive

12. and keep going, because that's what she believes

13. and that's the way the future is,

14. keep going, because she loves it (I love it)

15. and keep going when she can't do anything else (I dare to)

16. and keep going, because that's the whole idea.

17. That's the whole idea.

1. Got Mom and Dad from platform 2, Copenhagen Central Station, and they waved the whole way through the passenger tribe.

2. Let Dad tell everyone on the metro where he was coming from.

3. Let Mom hold my hand all the way home from Langgade Station.

4. Expected nothing less and said nothing about my expectations.

5. Took Valby from the green side, took Frederiksberg with flowers, wood pigeons, ducks, and Dad in the zoo,

6. *and it was the same animals they had in Central Park, I remember, penguins, polar bears, and wolves, and the stench of the primates' urine also the same, and I sat tailor-fashion like a local bohemian on a knoll with my takeaway and phoned Dad, who was walking about among his trees on the other side of the planet.* I can see the Empire State Building from where I'm sitting, *I lied.* And I can see the transformer tower, *he lied, and then we spoke for the rest about how long it had taken my postcard to get there.*

7. Had my picture taken with Dad and the cow with black patches.

8. Let Mom hold my hand, *and I didn't say a thing, and didn't cry either.*

9. Walked home through Søndermarken,

10. made them coffee while they rested their legs,

11. made notes about that when neither of them was watching, and then

12. let Dad tell everyone in the restaurant that it was my birthday.

13. Went home by Magnoliavej after dinner and the birthday business,

14. the lilacs, the California poppies, and Mom's fingers in my palm, quietly morsing the message, *It'll all turn out okay, it'll all turn out okay,*

15. it'll be okay,

16. my mother's fingers morsed, and then I morsed back

17. *Yes it will, yes it will.*

1. I was the Gefion Fountain, that was me it came from, and it flowed out across Central Station, the metro to Valby, and up the stairs to my flat, and the plash that sounded a bit after noon was me letting go in the hallway.

2. Tried not to drip on the table, even though I was filled with the sort of fluid you find in tear ducts, primordial soups, and amniotic sacs.

3. Went over the empty flat with a dishtowel.

4. Donned my running clothes, but was too beat to run and walked slowly with the sight of laburnum like a weight in my chest, *and I miss everything, if anyone can understand that.*

5. Fed a house sparrow from my hand and drowned it.

6. Got a call from Mom: *We're home now,* and that was that, and it wasn't that, it was more the entirety of it all, and everything that was lacking in order for life to proceed,

7. and then I walked home with my shoelaces untied and muddy.

8. Was in the shower without turning on the water,

9. sat slightly sweaty in the dusk,

10. *and it wasn't dangerous,* I reflected about my day as a baroque wetland. *It's just an aspect of the ability to love*

11. and thereby of love itself

12. and thus a sort of blessing.

1. Woke up one year older, feeling that this should be seen as a sign,

2. *but it isn't a sign of anything, other than that a day has passed.*

3. Paid my back taxes,

4. attended to my mail,

5. and took a long walk along the usual route through the cemetery to the elephants, and their mighty bodies played with each other in the pool as if they knew full well that their weight could prove fatal, and I stood there a long time, I stood at the side of an old woman who also pondered the elephants' love lives.

6. Bought scones at the good bakery on Gammel Kongevej

7. and sat down on the way home to read a book, not far from the grotto in Søndermarken, but was badgered by a duck that begged bread from park visitors, while the sweethearts on the blanket next to me were watching all the birds warily, including mine, because the woman was afraid of birds and because the man enjoyed defending her from them,

8. *and so we managed to pass the afternoon that way.*

9. Felt pain in my mouth,

10. pain in my lower back and the one hip,

11. walked slowly home

12. and opened all the windows, for it's a mild evening in Copenhagen,

13. and tomorrow I will maintain my faith in the day after tomorrow,

14. and that one day it will be me who's allowed to be there when the instruments are tuning,

15. for there comes a day,

16. and a day after that day,

17. that's the way days are.

1. Slept late,

2. went for a run,

3. lay down in bed and was awakened by the pigeons,

4. went for a bike ride after dinner to Western Cemetery and sat down someplace among the dead where no one could find me, and wished the evening the best, for that couldn't hurt.

5. Went home, because the mosquitoes began to bite, and made a cup of coffee,

6. stood there with the coffee in my hand,

7. stood there and my nose grew cold, it suddenly hit me,

8. *Perhaps I spend too much time in cemeteries,* I thought,

9. and lay down on the floor, vanished corporeally, *and if I don't exist, everything up to this point doesn't exist either, my history, America, the stone I walk around with in my pocket, and then what he wrote last winter,*

10. *and if none of those things exist, sorrow doesn't exist, and then tomorrow doesn't exist either,*

11. I thought, unable to breathe, *for that which doesn't exist cannot breathe,*

12. for there aren't many advantages to being that which doesn't exist, except for being able to walk through walls and listen at doors,

13. and I'd heard it all now, *so what is that?*

14. Got to my feet,

15. placed myself over by the window,

16. listened to one of the neighborhood dogs and stayed with it through thick and thin,

17. thought, *Why doesn't anyone let it in?* and could feel I was no longer a young woman,

18. just a woman who has lived longer than my neighbor and the dog down there and many of the dead, *and a thousand years ago I would have long since been laid in my grave,* I thought, *but look at me now,*

19. mournful, alive, and kicking,

20. and I'd like to be able to believe in tomorrow,

21. and I can't do anything but;

22. I'm hopelessly up the creek in the situation.

1. Sent my regrets,

2. thought about life's insistence on equilibrium: we lurch from side to side, *and for every time someone's caressed on the cheek, there's a place in the world where someone gets boxed on the ear, for every gleam of sunlight a shower of hail, for every door opened one closed, and thus for the heat that arises one place, somewhere else a new magnet is placed on the fridge.*

3. Scribbled down the line: *From her heart sprang the periphery of everything.*

4. Scribbled down the line: *Grow up!*

5. and tied a ribbon in my hair.

6. Went for a walk in the cemetery,

7. placed the petals from the first rugosa in my palm,

8. *and everything's dicey, but quiet.*

9. Thought that the worst thing about the things that change us for life, is that every day we have to persuade ourselves not to look at them and how they attest to the insignificance with which we're shuffled around, we're lost and found and lost again,

10. *these daily administrative actions,*

11. *even my pulse isn't sacred,*

12. *my family, my writing, my best intentions,*

13. *everything's dealt with,* I thought,

14. and tomorrow it's up and stand on your feet, stand and walk and bear the dead weight from place to place,

15. jump over the sun,

16. make contact with the universe

17. and continue on down to the laundromat.

1. Today I was visited by Kali.

2. Dropped things on the floor, wanted to split in half but couldn't,

3. *and I can't bear that this is a world where those who wreak damage are praised, and then today I'm visited by Kali.*

4. Felt the fury drawing up from the floor through my body like a soundless roar,

5. volcanic, huge, fragile.

6. Biked in to a friend's,

7. and then we were sitting there when a door slammed, and I, who'd tried all morning to get myself to cry, split before the eyes of another person, but it was no relief for she didn't know how to respond, and it's no good splitting and not being discovered, so I screamed the whole way home on the bike with the silence that civilization demands.

8. Made it home soaked to the skin, five miles in squall and downpour,

9. went through my keepsakes,

10. the written proofs,

11. and what should I believe among all the half-truths?

12. Wrote on the back of an envelope lying on the counter, *I'm angry, and not everything is art,* whereupon I picked all the magnets off the fridge and watered the clover on the windowsill,

13. shoved the dishes around as I washed them, because I hated doing them, just as I hated the deli counters in upscale supermarkets and the dog owners in Søndermarken, and I wanted to move back to Jutland and live in a henhouse and use empty beer cans for target practice, just to be close to something that seemed real, and dare to assume dance position and

lead myself around the floor, utterly alive, three-dimensionally present with pulse and all,

14. for I *will* exist, *So find me then, before I can't feel myself anymore,* I whispered out through my teeth, and then she found me, Kali, the angriest woman in the world,

15. and it isn't that I don't believe in the good in others.

16. It's that the others don't believe in the good in me.

1. Thought, *It's a long way from the dream of America to this,* and remained prone.

2. Thought about scabs and chamomile tea.

3. Couldn't make myself clear on the phone.

4. Couldn't stand other people, so I went out among them, and I walked past thousands but saw not one.

5. Reasoned, *Perhaps the part of me that once was in the US can still be found between the lines,*

6. but that isn't enough in the long run.

7. Went past the elephants, who were apparently doing well and, unaffected by anything, bathed in the pool and went on with their lives, trunk-flinging and backslapping, and on the way home I fainted in the cemetery behind a box hedge.

8. Cold sweat and hands asleep, *daisies.*

9. Remained prone afterward and relished the feeling of lost consciousness,

10. remained prone when the drizzle started,

11. remained prone until I could tell I was cold,

12. and then I got up and went out and looked for the next cemetery.

13. Reasoned, *International Women's Day would have torn me to shreds on the spot. But then it got me at last, and how many times do you have to hit out at a woman before she learns to duck?*

14. Bought a hot dog on Toftegård Square

15. and didn't want to go home, just to keep walking with the conviction that, if you keep walking, you'll come to a day where you're happy once more.

16. Reasoned, *Perhaps the part of me that once was in the US has been placed in a pantry in my mind, from where she can be retrieved again*

17. (but that isn't enough in the long run).

18. Walked home

19. and scribbled this down: *I am plagued by the vision of a faraway spring and my ability to read between the lines. I am a witness to my own truth in a flood of false evidence.*

1. Slept as though I were two people, and one of me awake.

2. Called Mom, without whom my nozzles would be shot.

3. Thanked Kali, whose rage had driven me a small piece of the way out of the fog, *this anxiety that reality will fail you, like late-night phone calls, cops at the door, others' perpetual worrying, and then you sit there and have to insist that you're doing it right and will manage, but after months of this you're weighed down with belief fatigue.*

4. Signed for a book and bore it from the post office through the supermarket and home.

5. Sang the same line again and again

6. and realized that, just because people aren't walking around with drips and catheters or lying in recovery position in bedrooms full of empties, it doesn't mean they're intact.

7. Went for a run, strong in the legs, as if Kali had given me some of her primordial soup,

8. *and it's spring now,*

9. and it is woman's weakness to believe it's because she isn't good enough that things don't go according to plan (and it is woman's weakness that things should go according to plan).

10. Envied all of them who looked as if they were in the catbird seat, on Queen Dagmar's Boulevard for instance,

11. people I hadn't heard from in years,

12. all of them who thought they knew better because they were doing better.

13. Wrote a thank-you note to Aunt Margrethe on the island of Fanø for the lovely amber necklace she'd sent

14. and sat there with Kali like a force in my body, for she's screamed me a piece of the way,

15. I'm on course to getting smarter,

16. I'm not nearly as empty-handed as yesterday,

17. and I am standing.

1. Went over the coded signs and symbols.

2. Brushed my teeth and ate my breakfast.

3. Sat down with a book on a bench in the cemetery and listened to the singing gibbons from the zoo and the raucous sirens in the distance, *and wounds are wounds, but not in the long run.*

4. Picked up a dried-out dog turd,

5. cast it away while I yelled, *To stifle things!*

6. and spooked the retired ladies in Park Cemetery, whose dogs leave turds behind in the general offcasting of everything in life that we don't want to bear around with us anymore

7. (but the soul has a long time horizon).

8. Scribbled down in the book's margin, *Diceyness is the worst,* and then walked home to go on reading,

9. read all that which was written there, as one reads a paper on the lookout for one's own obituary,

10. read as if the next subordinate clause might be my last, but I didn't die,

11. and then discovered myself, like a quiet tremor in the hand during winter, and I cast away anxiety, *for that which trembles in the hand one place is certainty in another, and diceyness is the worst.*

12. Thought, *If behavior made the globular woman at the pharmacy's breasts grow, then what might not be growing in me right now? My mind, my grief, my heart?*

13. Ate too many apples,

14. drank too much coffee,

15. so I'll have to go to sleep as if I were going to solve a rebus,

16. or I'll have to go to sleep as if I were two people and the other one awake,

17. I'll have to go to sleep with legs entangled in something,
18. between the falling manna and the desert sand
19. I am discovered, I am,
20. and therefore can sleep.

1. It's not the coffee that keeps me awake, it's Kali.

2. Tried to work, but Kali goes around grousing in the corners, jealous and insecure, pouting lips and all.

3. Did laundry.

4. Bought new running shoes.

5. Received a book for translation and leafed through the next month's work (while Kali grumbled), thought of Grundtvig (and Kali grumbled), wanted peace and quiet, wanted things brought back to earth (but Kali grumbled),

6. *and it isn't that I don't like being the goddess of death, but I can't stand still, I have to tromp on the floor in the laundromat, on the sidewalk, the grass, the ground,* I thought

7. and went for a walk in the cemetery while the clothes were in the tumbler, and Kali cast dog turds, and as for me I scribbled down this inscription from Landlord Frandsen's obelisk:

8. *Eternity lasts a long time,*

9. and I thought, *Everything is so lovely, even the cinquefoil's blooming,*

10. and then we stood there and looked at it, me and Kali, we looked at the cinquefoil, which didn't know any better (don't smite it, Kali),

11. but then she smote it, she smote it on the yellow petals

12. because it ought to have known better,

13. it might have known that,

14. that this was how it would turn out,

15. that it would turn out how it did,

16. it might have known

17. everything!

1. Was awakened by the heat.

2. Went to the flea market on Tullinsgade.

3. Watched a bagpipe band march through Værnedamsvej and continue out to the Vesterbro quarter, *and God knows where they are now.*

4. Was at the home of someone I know and not a peep from Kali, Kali just sat there while we looked at pictures and spoke of the sort of things that women can speak of, sunscreen and our time in the Women's Army Auxiliary, and in the absence of things to abuse, Kali took the back stairs and skedaddled, so I biked home alone.

5. Went for a run in the new running shoes,

6. ran, but fell at precisely the same spot where I'd always thought, *I'm going to fall there someday.*

7. Washed my knee off at the playground faucet, where kids were standing in line with their butts bare, and I stood in the back of the line like one of them, thinking scrapes were a chance to be comforted and expecting to pick off the scabs slowly soon afterward, and it would be a summer without short dresses.

8. Stopped by Vilhelm Kyhn's grave and looked at the birch tree that was planted over his coffin in 1903, bearing witness that Vilhelm Kyhn is extremely alive today.

9. Felt tired,

10. let things lie beside each other—

11. the frying pan, the dishrag, the joy, together with the insecurity and the French press; the shoes; the being inside, but outside, unseen, but discovered; the being hurt and the recovering, present, smarter, potentially happy, and entangled in will; and the dish towel— everything coordinated with a little prayer:

12. *Have patience and confidence until the end.*

1. Ate an apple in the middle of the night as the light seeped in over from Sweden.
2. Biked into Kastellet,
3. drank tea on a bench in the shade of a tree by one of the bastions,
4. plucked grasses and Queen Anne's lace,
5. made the dust rise on the paths
6. and looked at that bronze angel who wants to walk across the water to southern Sweden, *and it was chillier this winter,* I thought, *much chillier, and knowing that is something no one can take from me, but I can't share it, I bear it with me like a song stuck fast in the throat, like when I was supposed to sing "The Blessed New Day" for confirmation,*
7. and all that love has not been able to find peace since.
8. Watched a wooden ship squeeze into Copenhagen's harbor (as if it were long ago).
9. Watched a man eat his meal by himself at a restaurant on Borgergade (as if it were long ago).
10. Biked through the city, just one person on wheels among thousands of others on the way home to their own, exhausted and holding every conceivable unshareable thing inside,
11. rubbed the skins off new potatoes
12. and set the grasses in a vase on the counter,
13. thought of blackbirds and other singing creatures,
14. of all there's been, and tomorrow,
15. of my obligations, my dreams, my dusty sandals,
16. and then that which despite everything still calls,
17. *Come.*

1. Said, *Now you're going to take one day at a time.*

2. Said, *And this is the first of those days you're going to take one at a time*

3. and stood up then and had run out of milk.

4. Walked past the cemetery pigeons, *and it isn't that life goes on but that it'll never stop,*

5. was in the Frederiksberg Gardens,

6. hesitated by the pacifier tree and recalled Mom standing in a campground kitchen with a Swedish woman and a Dutch woman, the three of them busy looking into the bottom of a saucepan and taking ticks off some kid, *and I never offered up even a single pacifier to the pacifier tree on the path to the Chinese Pavilion.*

7. Bought a strawberry ice cream cone and couldn't grow up, no matter how much I might want to.

8. Took the words from my mouth and laid them in a small white coffin.

9. Read in the shade of a cemetery tree,

10. read page after page in the scent of warm box and felt pain in my tooth,

11. but that didn't matter.

12. Stopped by Kyhn's grave on the way back, *and it was the roses,*

13. *centifolia, multiflora, and Astrid Lindgren,* and there I stood and set aside everything I hoped for, and it was as if he turned his head from his verdigris bronze plaque and gazed down at me:

14. *Why, there we have you then, woman,*

15. *hoverflies about your face*

16. *and utterly alone.*

1. Stayed in bed taking another's downfall to heart,

2. and stones deliberately thrown in the other Zealand blazed through me as if on a sonar, *and now I don't know what I fear most: the sound of bones being crushed against the floor or things that rise up in the air, that which we never forget or that which we brush off, pistols against temples or threats pointed inward, the inertia of sorrow or its release.*

3. Promised to go to Tivoli (but declined the carousel in advance).

4. Went for a walk in the afternoon heat.

5. Had to stop frequently to rest a bit, for as soon as I feel alone inside, someone else steps on the stage.

6. Sat down by the goldfish pond,

7. thought of Indians, of clear skies and endless plantations. Thought of America, the heat, and another, of how I'd do violence to myself if I didn't revisit those places that I had, without much success, already afflicted with my plaints.

8. Longed for the smell of winter's cottages when they're opened up in June.

9. Longed for northwest Jutland and read poems in the shade,

10. wanted to forget everything I hadn't had, and which I should prepare to lose,

11. and chose the music on the lawn,

12. the soft ice cream and the helium-filled balloons,

13. the doubt, the sham happiness,

14. *for I don't know what I fear most, the sound of bones being crushed against the floor, or the sight of a child's hand letting go of the string on Bugs Bunny*

15. as easy as nothing.

1. Woke and rattled my arms.

2. Biked to the Open Air Museum in Brede.

3. Walked first thing into a house from Fanø, *and something's missing in this Zealandic heath—the local dances, the wading birds, or perhaps just Aunt Margrethe and a coffee machine.*

4. Went from house to house.

5. Inhaled the smell of a lost hay cutting and the sight of that feathered wing hanging above it all, *and I know I'm doing the right thing, and I know that it hurts (but just like birth, such things can be endured), I know that, just like I know that houses no one lives in no longer exist, and I want to exist.*

6. Used a toilet in the section on early industrialization.

7. Moved so slowly that I nearly stood still

8. and thought of the future, for you have to believe in it, thought of the past, because I could see it, thought of my memory and sat with it under an elderberry tree:

9. *and taciturnity's a form of protection,* I decided,

10. pinching off the heads of the wild chives that dangled about in the grass.

11. Watched a child crying after a run-in with a nettle bush by the double farmstead from southern Sweden,

12. felt pain in my tooth,

13. *but as we've seen, everything's just a transition phase,* I thought

14. and took Kongevejen home.

1. Woke knowing I would enjoy the surgical intervention, the painkillers, the cotton wads, the simplicity of scalpels, the body's transitory nature as the soul's lacerations persist and flap forever in the wind.

2. Had my last wisdom tooth extracted,

3. had my mouth stitched up with needle and thread by a man who said I would heal slowly because my age was against me,

4. *as if I didn't know that,* I thought, *as if it isn't such things that make me stop midmotion in plotting out the future, and if you've got something for aching of the heart, Dr. Lars, if you've got something for emptiness and loss of voice, if you've got something for time's tooth, then be sure to add it to my bill, but otherwise I think you should hold your tongue, unless you want to hear my philosophy of teeth—would you like to hear it? Would you?*

5. Didn't get the tooth to bring home.

6. Had to dismount several times from my bike to spit blood, *and I don't give a hoot, for in the midst of melancholy I am Kali, and Kali spits blood where she lists.*

7. Bought large quantities of ice cream.

8. Was knocked out by the painkillers.

9. Didn't waken till evening, when I sat up with a start: *Is this still the summer that would never end?* and then I felt my tooth, just because it'd disappeared.

10. Went for an evening stroll in the cemetery.

11. Decided to cast away the things that have plagued me for a long time, like my fridge, the failed effort, and, now that I was on a roll, the bleeding gums and inviolability,

12. *but I can't cast away the human being,* I thought, gazing at Snebjørn Gudmundson's gravestone with its doves and its birthdate in Reykjavik.

13. Cannot cast away recollection,

14. cannot cast away Brahms and those parts,

15. cannot cast away the memory and feeling and loss of my voice,

16. cannot cast away life, cannot cast it away.

1. Ran my tongue over the wound, and it was still there.

2. Sorted laundry, two piles, Tuesday.

3. Managed to exchange the wrecked sunglasses but could not exchange them for winter, no matter how much I wished to.

4. Concluded that what from my vantage appears to be the cold could well be something else,

5. *but on days when I fear disappointment, I prefer to look on the dark side of things, it pulls me together and keeps me one step ahead of suffering*

6. (and I shouldn't think that it won't continue either, for it does continue, day in and day out it continues, this hesitation that has taken me hostage, and it's going to be the longest summer ever, it'll be a summer that never lets go, and I'll end up being unable to distinguish it from last summer, which was precisely the same and kept on being so until the roses closed up from frost in the end of November, when I got the flu and a measure of peace).

7. Washed the floor and rinsed with chlorhexidine

8. and stood stock-still at the tail end of the afternoon and issued a sound that made all the dogs in Valby howl,

9. made the wound spring a leak, made me want to sing along, though I could not.

10. Went to yoga and assumed boat pose,

11. *and something must continue, though it cannot keep going,* I thought. *There must be an end to it. What we know and what we see before our eyes must merge and become one image. I want what I hold to be true and the magnets on the fridge to resemble each other,* I thought as I lay and pitched in the surf.

12. Biked home, called Mom to tell her,

13. *I want to have what's promised and what's living to make sense,*

14. and then she fell silent on the other end of the line,

15. as if she were stroking me indulgently on the cheek.

1. Woke to the throbbing in my mouth.

2. Sat up, thinking, *I can no longer remember a thing.*

3. Managed Stormgade on my bike,

4. found a place at the Royal Library and worked with the water behind me

5. and then discovered that the young man to my right in the reading room (as if in a piece of fiction) was busy reading a book about dental X-rays,

6. *and if it weren't because one's supposed to be quiet, I'd lean over and show him what I've lost, and I'd tell him how much it hurts, and then he could say something about the enamel and the cotton wads, whereupon we'd both have gone to lunch at Café Øieblikket that much the wiser.*

7. Drank my coffee in small sips with the view of Lange Bridge and recalled last winter,

8. recalled the gray light over Christianshavn, the way the mitten had gotten snagged on the banister, and I walked with my stollen back to my place, which vanished before me:

9. *I don't want to, I cannot, and you mustn't write me anymore,* he'd written,

10. nothing else,

11. and the time since had passed with knowing the difference between wanting and being able to.

12. Biked home with my dictionary and manuscript

13. to the small scraps of paper on my desk.

14. Went for a run in Frederiksberg Gardens and for a moment assumed that the ladder-to-heaven flowers were snowberries,

15. grew uneasy,

16. grew insecure,

17. *but then I remember the light in the kitchen, how the doors opened and the faces lifted, the dive of the bats, and that moment on the bench when the words in my mouth sat fast like that wisdom tooth, which until Monday sat fast in me and now is gone, and that was after America and before the birds settled in the grass, and I should have said that, I should have spit it out on the flagstones, like I've been spitting blood at present,* but that's the sort of thing you always know afterward, and I'm a woman, not an oral surgeon.

18. Tied my laces by the elephants.

19. Tied them again by the crematorium

20. and looked up and walked home

21. and could not forget a single thing.

1. Cut to the bone had it not been for the duvet.

2. Tried to work but was the whole time up on tenterhooks, down on my knees, back and forth on the floor.

3. Scribbled down my memoirs: *I couldn't help it.*

4. Scribbled them down again: *I was fragile, I was bone china,*

5. and I was Kali with a touch of Pippi and Pippi with a touch of the little match girl,

6. *and it isn't that I've got to contain them all in me, master and miniature alike, it's more that I shouldn't lose face during.*

7. Told Mom that it was unbearable, now that I've sat and waited so long in this waiting room: *So it's finally your turn, Miss Delicate, think you can still stand on those legs?* and when I called her up, it was because she was always the one who took me to the doctor when I was little, the one who asked, *Could you listen to the child's heart? Just to be on the safe side*

8. (and so I felt the cold metal against my skin, and the doctor moved the stethoscope across my chest in small hops as if my heart were in flight, for there isn't anything the heart fears more than people who listen to it of their own free will).

9. *There's a goodness besides the one you're waiting for,* said my mother. *So be patient,* she said,

10. and then I opened the windows to hear the Vietnamese neighbors' party in the backyard, *for happiness may well occur in ways we don't understand,* I thought, looking at the love I have and safeguarding it against enemy forces the way an Inuit guards his whale-oil lamp,

11. his mukluks,

12. and his laughter.

1. Grabbed the egg the second before it hit the floor,

2. went to the grocery store and dragged my little basket along

3. and took my place at the end of the line.

4. Fell into a reverie at the sight of the corpulent woman who is the supermarket's star cashier because the only thing she can do is move her arms, and they guide other people's everyday lives past the bar code reader so fast, you can hardly see the gold ring that shines on her finger, but it's there, and inside it says *Your eternal beloved*.

5. Bought new bulbs, since everything burns out anyway.

6. Decided that despite it all, I would stick to the truth as I knew it

7. and walked over to the cemetery,

8. and the pigeons rose into the air.

9. Discovered a gravestone of a person whom I knew to be utterly alive, and I'd walked down that path countless times but never seen the stone before, or in any case never noticed the name, *so perhaps it wasn't there yesterday, or there's another person buried there, or I just see my truths gradually as they unfold before me,*

10. I thought, and noticed that the person in question had died in 1934, and that it could therefore in no way be the same one, but other than that there was an absolute convergence of things that didn't make sense

11. and I felt humbled,

12. I felt listened to

13. and loved beneath the surface,

14. and bore in mind the thought that for God, a gravestone is just a scrap to make notes upon, the way the rest of us write our small concerns on the papers on the desk,

15. *and one thing is inescapable: I write,*

16. *I write*

17. *centifolia, multiflora, and Astrid Lindgren.*

18. *That cannot be changed,* I thought

19. and skirted the high-piled Midsummer Night bonfires, smiling (demented)

20. across the hay-scented lawns home.

Acknowledgments

I could not have written this book without the inspiration of those who came before me. *Minna Needs Rehearsal Space* was in particular inspired by the work of others. Above all I have to thank Ingmar Bergman. His books *Images: My Life in Film* and *Magic Lantern* live on in *Minna*. So do Jens Peter Jacobsen's 1874 poem "Arabesk: Til en Haandtegning af Michel Angelo" ["Arabesque: For a Drawing by Michelangelo"]; Bjørnstjerne Bjørnson's "Sangen Har Lysning" ["The Song Has Light"], also known as #159 in *Højskolesangbogen [The Danish Folk High School Songbook]*; and Carl Orff's "In Trutina" ["In the Balance"]. So grateful for your writing, dead guys. It was such an honor to sing duet with you on these pages.

Now to the living! I wish to express my gratitude to the Danish Arts Council and the Danish Arts Agency for supporting this book with grants. Thanks to my Danish editor Julie Paludan-Müller, and to my American editors Brigid Hughes and Fiona McCrae—and I can't forget the amazing Graywolf team and all the other great book people I work with in the US. A warm thank-you as well to Astri von Arbin Ahlander and Christine Edhäll in Stockholm (you rock!) and to the many writers and friends who have helped me find my way. A special thanks to translator Misha Hoekstra for his enthusiasm and extraordinary skill; it's been fun working with you. And last but not least: thank you to my family.

DORTHE NORS is the author of five books in her native Denmark, including the story collection *Karate Chop,* for which she received the 2014 Per Olov Enquist Literary Prize. Her work has appeared in the *New Yorker, A Public Space,* and *Harper's.* She lives in Jutland.

MISHA HOEKSTRA taught creative writing and literature at Deep Springs College before moving to Denmark in 1997. He writes and performs songs as Minka Hoist.

Book design by Ann Sudmeier. Composition by
Bookmobile Design & Digital Publisher Services,
Minneapolis, Minnesota. Manufactured by Versa Press
on acid-free, 30 percent postconsumer wastepaper.